BOOT

THE RUSTY RESCUE

HODDER CHILDREN'S BOOKS

First published in Great Britain in 2020 by Hodder and Stoughton

1 3 5 7 9 10 8 6 4 2

Text copyright © Shane Hegarty, 2020
Illustrations copyright © Ben Mantle, 2020

The moral rights of the author and illustrator have been asserted.

A CIP catalogue record for this book
is available from the British Library.

ISBN 978 1 444 94939 1

Printed and bound in Great Britain by
Clays Ltd, Elcograf S.p.A

The paper and board used in this book
are made from wood from responsible sources.

Hodder Children's Books
An imprint of
Hachette Children's Group
Part of Hodder and Stoughton
Carmelite House
50 Victoria Embankment
London EC4Y 0DZ

An Hachette UK Company
www.hachette.co.uk

www.hachettechildrens.co.uk

B◯◯T

THE RUSTY RESCUE

SHANE HEGARTY

ILLUSTRATED BY BEN MANTLE

For Aisling and Laoise.
Thanks for all the ideas
and inspiration.

BAD N⊛SE

The trouble started when Gerry's nose fell off.

Until then, it had been a normal day at Dr Twitchy's Emporium of Amusements. The sort of day I'd enjoyed a lot – thirty-six times, to be exact – since finding a new home here with robots just like me.

Robots who had been built to be clever, but who'd become even smarter than any human had expected.

Robots who had been unwanted or thrown out.

Robots who had given me help when I needed it most.

Robots who were now my friends.

Robots such as tough, almost indestructible Noke, who had first helped me when I was lost.

1

Noke was at the controls of an old mushroom-shaped carousel, its paint peeling and cogs creaking. The carousel hadn't worked for a long time, but my resourceful friend had fixed it.

"Are you ready for the ride of your lives?" asked Noke, watching me pull myself on to the swing, my backside in the air and my egg-shaped legs dangling over the edge. I wrapped the four fingers of each of my hands tightly around the chains.

"Are you sure it's fixed?" I asked, because the mushroom carousel had been rusty and stuck since before I arrived at Dr Twitchy's.

"It should run like a dream," said Noke, checking the control knobs.

"Will it be fun?"

"You'll giggle so much your head will fall off," said Noke.

I was sure Noke didn't mean my head would really fall off. Well, 98.71 per cent sure anyway.

"And will this be, you know, safe for all of us?" I glanced at another of my new friends, Red, who was chanting calmly on the swing beside me.

Red was the most beautiful and elegant robot I could ever imagine meeting, but was always in danger of getting too hot and catching fire if things got too stressful.

"Oh, you mean will it make Red burst into flames?" said Noke, twiddling some buttons.

"Let's keep this at a gentle speed, Noke," said

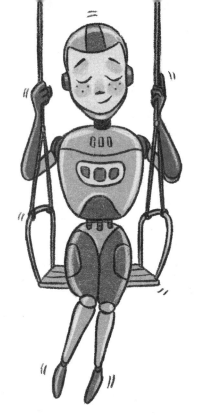

Red, in a low, sing-song voice. "Just enough of a breeze to cool my corners."

"I wouldn't mind some speed," said Gerry, wriggling about in excitement on the swing in front of me. "It would blow the cobwebs from my armpits. Spiders like my armpits."

Gerry had lived here a long time and had used a mishmash of things as spare parts. Gerry's right hand was the grabber from a claw machine. Both eyes were the revolving symbols from a fruit machine. And – for now – my patchwork friend's nose was a grubby ping-pong ball with two little dents in it where nostrils might be.

"So, let me get this straight," said Noke,

making a last check of
the controls. "You want
to go fast enough to
blow spiders from your
armpits, but not so
fast as to make anyone
explode. Got it."

As we waited for
the ride to start,
Poochy the electronic
dog zipped under the
swings and around my legs, barking glitchily.

"RUFF. RUPFFFIZZZITTTT."

Poochy wasn't smart like us. Poochy wasn't
smart at all, really. But it didn't matter. Poochy just
seemed to enjoy every moment.

After a loud, gritty crack of metal knuckles,
Noke called out, "Giddy-up!" and turned a dial.

The carousel lurched forward, starting up a
music-box lullaby.

We were off.

My swing lifted as the ride went around at a gentle pace. I felt a tickle in the circuits of my tummy, like fluffy feathers were floating about in there. I liked it.

With one eye flashing brightly, Poochy scampered around the wooden floor beneath our feet, skirting the exposed cogs and gears at the centre of the ride.

"RUFF. RUFFTTZZZPPTT."

The lullaby played as the swings rose and we revolved at a nice speed.

I burped a giggle.

Red smiled, while humming a low, calming tune.

"This *is* fun," I said. My cartoon face burst into bright, orange happiness.

I was with my new friends, in my new home, in my new life.

This was wonderful.

The carousel turned a little faster. Then faster still. Then a little too fast.

The lullaby played at a faster pace too, sounding less like a gentle lullaby and more like a jig.

My tummy got a bit ticklier.

"This speed is making me a bit too warm," said Red.

"It won't go any faster, will it Noke?" I called.

"Don't worry – just a bit faster and a few more thrills, but no exploding!" Noke said, turning up the dial.

Poochy's rusty little legs were working as fast as they could to keep up with the moving floor.

"My head is rattling," shouted Gerry.

The lights of Dr Twitchy's began to blur

a bit. Even though my sensors can see the smallest details, the colours were now becoming a whirl in my vision.

"Time to stop the ride, Noke," called Red, beginning to redden a little.

"Fair enough," said Noke, placing both hands on the controls. "Oh. Hold on a second. The dial's a bit stiff …"

As we sped past, we saw the dial come off in Noke's hands.

"Oops."

My tummy didn't feel like it was being tickled by feathers now. It felt like it was full of worms.

"Please stop!" I begged.

"I can't!" said Noke.

I clung on tight to the chains. Was I going to be flung across the room and into the row of old arcade games opposite? My circuits and wires would be sent to every corner of Dr Twitchy's. My head would be used as a bowling ball. My legs would be the bowling pins!

The little dots of light that made up my face

spread across my screen like a smudge. I couldn't hold on much longer.

"My nose!" shouted Gerry.

A white blob shot towards my face.

Gerry's ping-pong-ball nose had come free. It *pinged* off my head and bounced off the floor.

In a blur of fur, Poochy leapt up and snatched the ping-pong ball from the air.

"I'm trying to fix the dial!" shouted Noke from the controls. "No. I can't fix the dial!"

We were in big trouble.

"Don't bite my nose!" Gerry cried at Poochy as we whizzed around faster and faster.

RUFF, RUFFTTSSPPST! said Poochy, flinging the ping-pong ball away.

It plopped right into the gears at the centre of the carousel.

And was crushed.

"My beautiful nose!" said Gerry.

With a loud CREAK, a couple of SNAPS and a

sound that was like a *GGGGRRRROOOAAA
AAANNNPPPPPKKKK* the ride came to a
halt, leaving us bouncing about on the swings.
The lullaby song skipped twice, slowed and
stopped.

Gerry's nose was wedged in the gears of the
carousel. It had saved us!

I wobbled off the swing. My legs went one way.
My body went another. I couldn't tell *where* my
brain was going.

I stumbled down from the ride, on to the floor
and fell on my back.

Red stood over me looking, well, worryingly *red.*

Gerry pulled the crushed ping-pong ball from
the gears. "I *need* a nose. When bits fall off me I
don't feel complete. I'm just a broken robot ... A
broken robot with no nose."

Gerry pressed the squashed ball back into place
and came over to where I was lying. "Be honest,
how does it look now?"

The squished ball fell sadly to the ground.

Gerry groaned loudly.

Free of the ping-pong ball, the carousel had
started to move again. Its tinkly lullaby rang out
but sounded sickly now.

Noke appeared above me and offered a hand to
get me up.

"Was it terrifying?" asked Noke, as I got to my
feet unsteadily. "It *looked* terrifying."

I thought hard and put my cartoon face back
together in the right order.

I nodded.

"Sounds like my kind of fun. I'm going to fix the dial and have a go," said Noke and bounded off to the swings.

I felt the crack on my screen to make sure it hadn't widened. That crack was part of my story – something I'd woken up with before I went looking for my owner, Beth – but I didn't want it getting so wide that my screen fell off.

I checked my hip, opening the little drawer I had there. The drawer was still in one piece. More importantly, a red jewel given to me by Beth – one from the butterfly pendant that had helped me find her – was still inside.

I closed the drawer and checked over the rest of my body for bumps or bangs. I had definitely been bumped and banged, but nothing seemed dented.

"My system has heated up to dangerous levels," said Red, sitting upright on a bench by the pinball machine, hands on knees, eyes closed. "I need to cool down. And I *need* to avoid thrills."

"I *need* a nose," groaned Gerry, examining the crumpled ping-pong ball.

This was not the first time Gerry had needed a new nose. Gerry had already tried a tap, a bath plug, an old sock, a door key, and even a chocolate bar. The chocolate nose hadn't lasted long, thanks to hot weather. And a hungry rat.

"Remember the time I tried a balloon nose?" Gerry said.

"Oh yeah," said Noke, going by on the carousel. "That idea blew up in your face!"

"Don't remind me," said Red.

"If I stop replacing my parts, then what next?" continued Gerry, upset. "Just let my head drop off and roll away?"

"You need a proper robot nose, to stop this

happening again," said Noke, circling back around on the carousel, feet up in the air.

"Will you give me yours?" asked Gerry hopefully.

"No can do," called Noke. "It's my best feature. That and the way the light reflects off the screws in my eyebrows."

"Can't we find one somewhere?" I asked.

"If you hadn't turned up the speed, this wouldn't have happened," said Red, eyes still closed. "You kind of owe Gerry a nose, Noke."

Noke passed around again. "All right. You've got me there, Red. There is one place ... Gerry knows where it is."

"Oh no," said Gerry, shoulders sagging.

"It's our best bet," called Noke.

"I know, but—"

"You don't

have to go in there, Gerry. You only need to show us where to go."

I had no idea what they were talking about. But before I could ask, Gerry said a reluctant, "OK."

With a long "WHEEEEEEEE", Noke flew off the swings, bounced along the ground and knocked into an old jukebox that started playing ancient pop music.

"Right then," Noke said, getting up. "Who's coming to the Testing Lab?"

WALK LIKE A R⚙B⚙T

Before long, we were rolling through the city streets in a barrel robot, bumping and bashing and jolting against each other. Gerry's elbow was on my leg and Poochy's tail wagged across my face like a windscreen wiper. Red had decided to stay at Dr Twitchy's, to avoid overheating any more.

A barrel robot was a useful way to travel because it allowed us stay hidden from people when we wanted to. Unclaimed robots could be grabbed by humans, which had nearly happened to me before I came to Dr Twitchy's. A man named Flint had chased me, so he could throw me back in to the grinder I'd escaped from.

I didn't want that to happen again. The grinder would do to me what the carousel had done to

Gerry's ping-pong-ball nose.

"Maybe we'll call a taxi next time," said Noke, whose knee was on my chest. "Those robot cabs will only take orders from humans, but I know how to put my magic finger in the right places and get them to go where I want."

The barrel stopped with a jerk and Noke's 'magic finger' poked me in the ear.

Noke slid the door open, letting in a blast of daylight and allowing us to wriggle free for a few moments.

We were at a pedestrian crossing. The noise of the city made my brain shudder. Vehicles passed by on the road, drones flew through the air. People moved around us, all of them talking to these big, sophisticated, sleek robots with information scrolling around the screens of their faces.

"They think they are so intelligent and sophisticated, but they're just zombie-brains," said Noke.

"Yes, I'm glad we're not like those robots," I said.

"Not the robots," said Noke. "The humans!"

A little girl held her mother's hand as they approached the crossing. The mother was only paying attention to her robot, whose face flashed with pictures and messages. But the little girl peered into the barrel at us.

Noke pulled an eyebrow off and wore it like a moustache.

The child squealed with laughter.

I burped a giggle.

The lights changed at the junction, Noke slid the barrel door closed again and we moved on.

Seeing the girl laugh had felt good.

I had been a toy once, until I woke up in a grinder with a crack on my face and only two-and-a-half memories of where I came from. In the end I found my old owner, Beth. She was visiting the elderly care home where her grandma now lived.

Beth was kind and lovely but she saw that I'd changed so much. That I was no ordinary 'Robot-O-Fun, your Favourite Funtime Pal' any more.

I was *me*.

Beth had given me back my memories. I remembered my time with her – every sunrise, every night-time, every good day, every bad, every bit of fun, every bit of trouble, all the times we played together, every time I was tucked up under Beth's arm, or dressed in crazy clothes, or asked to do a ridiculous dance.

I remembered being the birthday gift that made Beth yell with delight. I remembered the happier times with her grandma. I remembered every single time I made them laugh together.

Yes, I was *me* now. But I had so enjoyed being Beth's Favourite Funtime Pal.

"We're here," announced Noke.

The barrel door opened and we were all tipped out on to a concrete path in a pile of robot legs and arms.

"**RUFF,**" said Poochy. "**RUUFFFZZZTT.**"

"My arm feels loose," said Gerry. "Is my arm loose? Are my eyes about to fall out?"

Getting to my feet, I saw we were at the edge of the city. In the distance, the great skyscrapers reflected the sun, and from this far away, the drones that flew between them looked like buzzing flies.

Before us loomed an imposing block of a building, a windowless, unwelcoming place made of grey brick that stretched several storeys high.

It was so wide either side that it was hard to see where the walls ended and the equally grey road began.

The only way in seemed to be through large, shuttered doors – I counted twelve of them – lined up along the wall. Each one was closed.

"Here it is," said Gerry, nervously. "The Testing Lab. This is where humans test all the new stuff that will be sold in shops. Things like dishwashers, sofas, blenders, microwaves, toys, toilets, electric toothbrushes – you name it."

"I met an electric toothbrush once," said Noke. "Wasn't very chatty."

There was the sound of a vehicle approaching from the road we'd rolled up. It was a bus, rattling towards us with occasional belches of black smoke and groans of its engine.

Gerry tugged at my arm and the four of us scuttled behind our barrel robot. Peeking over the top, we watched the bus get closer until it stopped just short of the door next to us.

"The humans need someone to test these things," continued Gerry. "Someone who'll do the same job over and over and over again until the thing they're testing breaks. Or *they* break."

The bus doors hissed and swung open.

This place felt creepy. I didn't like it.

"And because humans don't want to do that job themselves, they use robots. But ..." Gerry seemed to be finding it difficult to talk about this, "... they don't use just any robots."

A metal leg appeared from the bus door, attached to the body of a large robot with all its wiring exposed. It was missing one arm.

It was followed by another robot, this one with a badly dented domed head on a short body attached to mini tank tracks, so that it moved off the bus step like a snail.

One by one, robots emerged from the bus. Some were wide, others squat. Some had legs, some had wheels. One had a several legs like a spider.

Some of the robots were solid and tough, while others were slender and looked fragile. But they had one thing in common. They were all broken in some way.

Some had cracks in their bodies. Some had limps from malfunctioning legs, or arms that hung by their side, not working, or screens that glitched and froze.

One robot – tall and sleek like the robots we saw so often with people on the street – rocked forward and back while repeating a single word over and over. "**LIKE, LIKE, LIKE, LIKE, LIKE** ..."

Gerry's voice turned low and sad. "Sometimes, when a robot is being made in the factory, something goes wrong. A limb is loose, or there's a glitch in their programming. Or they're missing important parts."

"Rather than let them go to waste, the humans send the broken robots here to do the testing work," said Noke.

"I ... I ... I was one of these robots," Gerry whispered, looking ashamed.

Poor Gerry. I was a little broken too. I traced the crack on my face. I touched the drawer at my hip, remembering a memory from when I lived with Beth and it snapped out when I accidentally fell off her bike.

She had been so upset, but her dad had fixed it. Carefully. Calmly. Telling her I'd be as good as new. And I was.

"But you escaped, right Gerry?" said Noke. "They didn't know you were clever. Different. Special, like us."

The testing robots had lined up in threes, facing the door.

"When I was brought here, and waited outside with all the other broken robots, I heard some of the human workers talking all about this place," said Gerry. "About how the robots worked here until they broke completely. How when that happened the robots just took themselves off to be scrapped."

I knew what it was like to be almost scrapped. I couldn't imagine just walking into that myself.

"Something in my brain told me I had to get out of here," continued Gerry. "That I wasn't to be one of *those* robots. I had to leave before it was too late. So I escaped."

The Testing Lab shutters rolled up with a rhythmic clatter.

"Here's our chance," said Noke.

"These robots will be sent to Testing Rooms," Gerry said, hurriedly. "Follow one of them and once you're inside, look for a robot that's already been doing a job for so long it's about to fall apart."

Fall apart?

"When it does fall apart, it'll lead you to where all the scrapped robots go. And the spare noses. But be careful. Please."

Noke placed a hand on Gerry's shoulder. "You stay here and mind the barrel robot. We'll bring you back the most glorious nose we can find."

Gerry's eyes spun at that promise.

"Poochy, you come with us. You might be useful in case we need to get into anywhere small," said Noke.

"RUFF. RUFFFZZPPPTTT," barked Poochy.

"And Boot," said Noke, putting a hand on my shiny shoulder and pulling me out into the open and into the line of robots. "It's time to act like a robot."

But we are robots, I thought. My face went blank with confusion.

"Perfect!" said Noke.

The lines of robots began to walk mindlessly towards the entrance. Beside me, Noke faced forward and started marching stiffly. Poochy darted giddily in and around the lines and disappeared out of sight.

There was no time to find where the dog had gone, because a man in brown overalls appeared at the Testing Lab's wide door, holding a clipboard and inspecting the arriving robots.

I suddenly realised that was why Noke wanted us to act like the other robots. We couldn't stand out.

I did my best to match Noke. I walked stiffly, drew blank eyes and a straight mouth on my screen, tried not to say or do anything that would give us away.

Just in front of us, a golden robot with short bent legs under a tall boxy body wandered out of the line. The man kicked it. "Straighten up, bolts for brains."

The line stopped for a moment to let the golden robot step back in. I was concentrating so hard on walking like a robot I didn't react quickly enough and thudded into the back of the robot with spider legs. Hearing the thud, the man walked over to inspect.

I tried to look as blank as possible.

The man stared so closely at me his breath fogged the corner of my screen. Out of the edges of my vision I could see he had hair growing from his nostrils, which is a weird thing some men like to do.

He tapped me on my face with his pen. It took all my little strength not to run away with fright. What if he realised I wasn't broken like the other robots? What if he realised I was clever? What if he took me to the grinder?

The man grunted. "You look like a particularly

34

stupid machine," he said. "Maybe with that crack in your screen, we'll send you to the face-punching room. You're perfect for testing boxing gloves."

Face-punching room?

"**LIKE, LIKE, LIKE, LIKE, LIKE, LIKE** ..." the sleek, tall robot jabbered.

This distracted the man with the clipboard and the line started to move on again. I moved with it, swaying like a robot, my arms by my side. I added a limp to look even more broken. I thought I felt the man watching me, but he left me to march on until the line entered the doors of the huge building.

"Good job," Noke whispered to me. "You make a convincing robot,"

We marched into a wide gleaming corridor that led from the entrance. Glass sliding doors stretched along the corridor and the broken robots began to step out of the line and through these doors, into tube-like elevators.

They would wait a moment and then –

SCHLUMP – they'd shoot up the tubes.

I wanted to curl into a ball and roll away, but I stayed in step with Noke, walking as awkwardly as I could. Noke followed a large, limping robot out of the line and towards one of the tubes – so I went too.

"Where's Poochy?" I asked Noke quietly.

A hatch in the bottom of the limping robot opened and Poochy's head popped out.

"RUFF," said Poochy. **"RUFFFTTZZPPTTT."**

"Are we sure this is where we should go?" I asked Noke.

"My instinct never fails me," said Noke confidently as we stood with the large robot in the tube. "And my instinct says we should go that way."

Noke pointed up to the dark of the tube above us.

I heard a gathering roar of air. Poochy quickly

returned back inside the large robot and then, with a sudden **SCHLUUUMP**, they were both sucked roughly up the tube.

Before I could ask Noke if this was a good idea, my head felt a drag of air, my legs hovered off the ground and – **SCHLUUUMP!** – I was gone too.

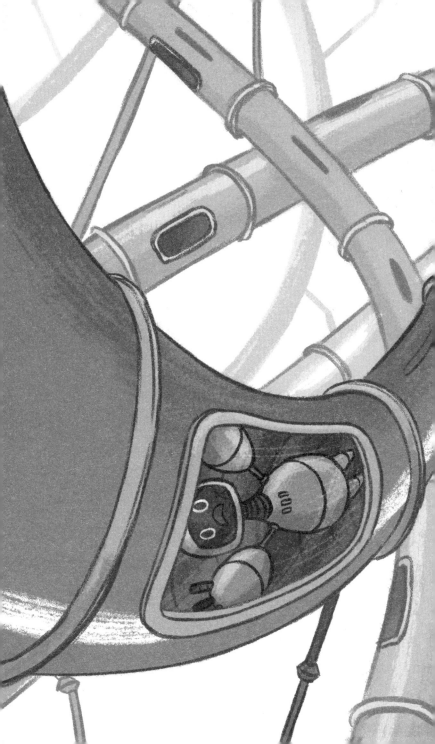

TESTING R✹✹M 101

My body bounced and banged against the walls of the smooth tube as I was sucked helplessly along.

I shot up, then around a bend, then down a bit and up a lot more. I pushed out my hands to try and stop but couldn't. I wished I wasn't here. I wished I was back in Dr Twitchy's. I wished I hadn't gone looking for Gerry's nose.

And then, as suddenly as I'd been sucked into the tube, the air quietened and I slowed, stopped and found myself floating a moment. At this spot, the tube went in two directions – up further, or across.

Puffs of air guided me across and I floated gently out of the tube and on to the floor in a corridor. The large limping robot was there already.

"RUFF," barked Poochy from the hatch in the robot's backside.

"RFFFPPZZTTT."

From back inside the tube, I could hear a shouted "Yee-hah" getting louder as Noke zoomed towards us.

Floating out and landing next to me, Noke declared, "This place is *great*!"

I pointed at my friend's left ear, which had come loose. Noke smacked it back into place.

Was this place great? I didn't *feel* great. Thanks to the tube, I felt like my insides had been stuffed into the top of my head and my legs had been turned upside down.

I looked around. The corridor we'd landed in was lined with doors, each of which had a window. There was a sign above each door. The one nearest us said:

TESTING ROOM 99:
KITCHEN APPLIANCES

Stretching as tall as I could on my little legs, I peered through the window and saw a very strange sight.

It was a kitchen, much bigger than the one in Beth's home. There was a cooker and a fridge, a microwave and a blender, a dishwasher and a

41

sink, all arranged along a black countertop. And it was filled with robots. Like the ones we'd seen outside, they were of different sizes and shapes and materials, and each of them had a flaw of some sort.

One robot twitched and glitched every few seconds, spitting sparks from its mouth. Another was missing a foot and rested on the frayed wires exposed at its ankle.

But each of them had a job to do. Just one job.

One opened the fridge door and closed it again. Then again. And again.

Another lifted a frying pan on and off the stove, flipping an imaginary pancake each time.

A robot whirred the blender for a few seconds, let it calm and then whirred it again. One boiled a kettle. Another turned a tap on and off and on and off and on and—

PING! A robot opened a microwave door.

Beside each robot were counters, ticking over

each time the robot did their job. The microwave had gone *ping* 102,991 times already.

PING! 102,992.

"This place is even weirder than I imagined," said Noke, joining me at the window. "And I can imagine really *weird* things."

We moved to the next door.

TESTING ROOM 100:
BEDROOM (CHILDREN'S)

The room looked a bit like a child's bedroom but wasn't *right*. It certainly didn't have the cosiness of Beth's bedroom. Her floor used to be littered with books, clothes, toys. She had posters on the wall and cuddly teddies piled high. It was comfortable and lived in. It was a *home*.

This was not a home.

This room had a bed, but a robot with a missing head was jumping on it, over and over.

It had jumped 212,250 times and the bed was
sagging heavily in the middle.

Another robot played a child's keyboard
carelessly, just smacking at the keys. The edges of
the plastic keyboard had chipped and broken from
overuse. Its stand looked like it might buckle at
any moment.

A small robot – even smaller than me – shook a snowglobe with a little castle in it. Let it settle. Shook it again. It had done that 27,018 times already.

My cartoon mouth was a round 'O'. Not of shock or surprise, even though I did feel that, but of a sort of sadness for these poor robots stuck in there.

"These robots are not like us, are they?" I asked Noke.

"I really hope not," said Noke, moving to the next window. "Ah-ha, this might be what we need …"

Noke pushed open the door to

TESTING ROOM 101:
LIVING ROOM

Inside this room, four robots were arranged like a family might be in a normal living room.

A spindly robot with a crack right down its body ran a vacuum cleaner back and forth over a rug that was worn bare.

A short, round robot – its face and body all one, with arms and legs sticking out either side – was slumped on a huge beanbag. It held a game controller, twiddling the little joystick and thumbing the buttons.

"Look at this one," said Noke, waving a hand in front of the face of a robot that stood before a TV set with a remote control, flicking through the channels.

Flick. Flick. Flick.

The TV ran through cartoons, news bulletins, nature shows and a programme with a woman who got very excited when she made a cake shaped like a cactus.

Noke closely examined the robot's fingers and beckoned me to do the same. They looked worn down, their silver coating flaking away, two knuckles popping loudly every time the robot changed channel.

I looked up into the robot's eyes. One was cracked, and a little leak of oil was dribbling from the eye socket and down its cheek.

But it didn't look back at me. It just kept flicking through football, alligators, a cartoon about people made of cheese.

A counter beside it ticked up speedily. 1,040,177 … 1,040,178 …

I was not sure I had ever been bored. But if I had been stuck in one of these Testing Rooms, doing the same job over and over and over, I knew for sure I would have seized up from being very, *very* bored.

"Gerry told us that one of two things is going to happen here," explained Noke. "Either the remote control will break, or the robot's fingers will drop off. If the fingers go, then the robot will take itself to the place where *really* broken robots go. We'll find all the noses we need there."

"But that could be a while," I said.

"I don't think we'll have to wait too long," said Noke, pointing at an imposing, triangular-shouldered robot in the very corner of the room. "I spotted that huge rusty-looking robot through the window. It looks like it's on its very last legs."

This was one massive robot, with thick knee hinges and bolts fatter than my fingers. Its shoulders were wide and its head was hardly a proper head at all, more like a tin helmet put on top of the shoulders.

Its eyes were square torches with dirty bulbs. Its mouth was a line of seven bulbs, none of them lit, squeezing up against its eyes and leaving no room for a nose.

The robot slowly sat on a leather chair. With great effort and creaking and what sounded like a deep, rattling groan, the robot stood up. Then, with just as much effort, it sat down again.

Each time it did this, it shed a fine spray of rust – which settled around the robot's feet in a dull red circle.

The counter beside it told us the robot had sat on the chair 761,578 times.

"My instinct tells me this rusty one won't last much longer," said Noke.

It was broken too, its right arm floppy and hanging longer than the other, with wires showing at the shoulder and its elbow hinge snapped and twisted.

The big robot stood again with effort, a creak and a rattling from somewhere deep inside, while its broken arm sagged uselessly.

"Sorry …" I said to it, my face turning a deep blue of sadness. I didn't really know why I said that. It just felt like the right thing to do.

The robot turned and looked down at me, its neck scraping and a couple of flakes of rust dropping free.

I stepped back in surprise. There was something in the large bulbs of its eyes. Something unlike all the other robots here.

A shadow moved across the window.

The huge robot looked away again and continued its job.

"Someone's coming!" hissed Noke.

A woman in brown overalls shoved the door open with her shoulder while examining a clipboard.

"Think quick!" said Noke, dropping to the ground and wedging under the game-playing robot's beanbag.

Think quick? I always thought at the same speed, but everything was muddled right now.

The woman walked through the room towards us, flipping pages on her clipboard.

The large robot sat on the chair again, its joints creaking.

I needed a really clever plan to look like I was

just another robot doing a terrible, repetitive job until I broke.

The robot stood again, with a chest-rattling sigh.

I didn't have a clever plan. So I just rolled into a ball and scooted underneath the soft chair, popping my head out to watch through a hole in the fabric.

I thought I heard the robot grunt before it sat again – was it surprise? – then I felt its full weight on top of me as it sank into the dangerously worn-out chair.

The woman was right beside us now. "You are a persistent hunk of junk," she said to the triangle-shouldered robot. "I can't believe you've not gone to Robot Heaven yet." She laughed, the pen scratching at her clipboard.

The big robot didn't answer. Of course it didn't. It just got up again. And sat down again. A fine dusting of rust fell gently to the floor at its feet.

I had to remain calm and quiet, even though

I was afraid of being crushed, or falling apart, or being caught. Or all three. I wished I had a switch to turn off my fear.

"Hahaha, Robot Heaven," the woman laughed. "Where spare parts fall like rain."

She turned away. I saw the tips of Noke's rubber feet sticking out from under the bean bag and hoped she didn't see them too.

"Stupid machines," she tutted, while ticking

off a list. "Just doing the same dumb job over and over until they die."

The hulking robot was pressing down on me so hard.

DANGER! flashed in my vision.
DANGER!

"Danger!" I said. I didn't mean to. I couldn't help it. It escaped from me by accident.

The woman turned back, her feet right up against the base of the chair.

"Excuse me?" she said.

The big robot just kept doing its job. I kept trying to be quiet.

"Did you say something? Or is there someone under there?"

The woman bent down to have a look.

I was going to be found.

I was going to be scrapped.

Gerry would never get a nose.

There was a clatter behind her. The game-playing robot's finger had fallen off. The robot dropped the controls, which bounced on to the floor. The game burst into a long, unbroken electronic beep, like it was complaining.

The woman straightened up and turned back towards it. As if knowing its time was up, the game-playing robot rolled forward off the beanbag into a standing position.

A square door slid open in the nearby wall. Peering out from under the chair, I could just about see it led to a chute. The game-playing robot simply flopped headfirst into the chute and disappeared. The woman threw the broken finger in after it.

That was our way out. And the way to a nose for Gerry!

The door to our room opened and the robot Poochy had hidden inside walked into our room and towards the game.

Before it got there, Noke squeezed out from

under the beanbag and pointed at the chute in the wall. "Looks like we've found the place where really broken robots go."

The woman dropped her clipboard down and stared at Noke.

"Oh," said Noke. "*You're* still here."

The big robot was about to sit again. I suddenly panicked. The woman had seen Noke and I needed to get out before I was squashed.

My circuits must have glitched from the rush of
feelings, because I popped open and tore through
the centre of the worn-out chair. With a crunchy
splinter, the whole thing fell in on itself.

The woman gasped.

Poochy jumped out of the bottom of the tall,
slim robot. He was biting down on a metal part
that looked almost like a silver bone.

The woman screamed.

The great robot above me stopped halfway into a sitting position, its knees creaking with the strain. It looked down at me again. Its eyes brightened and dimmed as if it was trying to understand what was happening.

The counter beside it flipped all its numbers and reset to ZERO.

The woman ran to the door, half-tripping over the vacuum cleaner still being pushed by its robot, and smacked an alarm button as she left hurriedly. A wail of bells rang through the whole building.

"She's going to be back with help," said Noke. "Come on, Boot! We just need to find a nose for Gerry and get out of here before they start doing tests on *us*."

I started for the chute but couldn't help but look back at the big rusty robot, hovering over the collapsed chair halfway between sitting and standing.

"Chair. Broken," it said in a soft, forlorn voice

that rattled up from deep within. A bulb in its mouth flickered as it spoke. "You broke it."

This robot was not like all the others. This robot was like *us*.

I could *not* leave it behind.

BR⚙KEN

Jumping to the chute, Noke stopped its doors from sliding shut. "Boot, we need to go before the humans come back with things far more dangerous than clipboards!"

The alarm rang through the building. Poochy stood between me and Noke, head cocked and biting firmly on the metal bone, waiting for me to go.

But I couldn't go.

I couldn't leave this robot behind.

"You broke my chair," it said. "What will I do now?"

"I'm being squeezed like an orange," said Noke, using as much strength as possible to keep the door open for me. "So come on!"

"I'm sorry I broke your chair," I said to the robot.

It looked at the broken pieces of the chair and back at me. Every movement looked and sounded tired.

"Everything," it said. "Sitting. Standing. Gone."

"Do you know what's down this chute?" said Noke, sounding quite desperate now.

The robot stood fully before answering. "Robot Heaven."

"Oh yes, where spare parts fall like rain," said Noke. "Then let's go there before the humans arrive to turn us into spare parts."

The alarm bells were ringing so loudly it felt like my screen was shaking.

"You don't have to stay here," I told the big robot. "You can come with us."

"Didn't finish my job," said the robot, examining the wreckage of the chair. "You broke my chair."

"You aren't like the other robots here," I said, as calmly and as encouragingly as I could, even though every circuit in my body was telling me to run away in a panic. "You're clever like us."

"Not clever. Not good," said the robot with a slow shake of the head and a shoulder swivel that brought its limp right arm swinging across its chest. "I'm broken. Only good for sitting on the chair. My chair is broken."

"I'm getting very squashy!" said Noke, sounding very squashy.

"Come with us," I said.

"RFFFF," said Poochy, **"RFFPPSSSTTT."**

"My chair ..." repeated the robot. It seemed stuck in that thought, like it had no idea at all what to do next.

I felt so bad about breaking the chair and about everything this robot must have been through.

I heard people outside in the corridor, getting closer.

"We have an old amusement arcade," I said.

The robot didn't move.

"We live with other robots, just like us," I added.

"Boot! We *have* to go," said Noke, firmly.

Poochy did a forward roll and landed under Noke's legs.

I wasn't leaving without this robot. It wouldn't be right.

And then I had an idea.

I smacked my belly and a hologram popped up between us. It showed a metal bench from Dr Twitchy's.

"We have chairs! *Lots* of chairs."

"Will they break if I do my job?"

"No …" I said. "Maybe. Whatever would make you happy."

The door into the Testing Room burst open and the clipboard woman stood there with four more humans behind her. She pointed at us. "There they are. Whatever *they* are!"

The robot looked at her, looked at me, looked

at the broken chair, looked at the hologram, then, with a shuffle towards Noke, it opened the doors in the wall with its good hand.

"That's a relief," said Noke, gently backheeling Poochy down the chute and following after.

"Don't go anywhere!" shouted the woman as the humans rushed towards us.

"We should go now," I told the robot, urgently.

Together, we dropped into the wide chute. I had no idea what was waiting for us at the end.

THUMP AND SMASH

We slid down a long curving chute in complete darkness.

I turned the torch in my screen to full beam to see where we were sliding and crashed straight into the back of my new robot friend, who seemed to be stuck.

I heard voices echo down the chute from the room above.

"They're still rattling about in there. I'd say they're stuck," said a man's voice. It was the man we had met outside, the one who grew hair in his nostrils.

"We should send down a Clear-Out Bot," said the woman.

"Good idea," said the man. "That'll shred 'em.

Get the chute clear."

Shred?

The chute was wide, but this bulky robot must have been wider.

"Try and waggle your shoulders," I suggested, as quietly as I could.

It didn't budge.

I heard something scuttle down the chute behind us, and the loud whirr of propellers. Slicing propellers, I guessed. I was sure they would make mince-metal out of me if we didn't move soon.

As the chute began to shake, I clambered up on to the robot's shoulders and looked over to see what might be blocking the way. I flashed an exclamation mark on my face when I realised what the problem was.

The robot was actually holding on to the chute with its one working arm.

"Why are you doing that?" I asked.

"I'm scared," it said.

"You need to let go," I said. "We'll be chopped up."

"My chair is broken. What if there's no Robot Heaven for *me*?"

The clear-out robot was getting closer, its noise like a jet engine. The chute began to rattle violently.

"I know you're scared," I said, trying to stay calm even as I could feel the whoosh of propellers pushing the air towards us. "I felt the same way once. But I promise with good friends and a home like we have, there's nothing to be scared of."

"Nothing to be scared of?"

My brain began to count up the many, many things to be scared of. But I just nodded and beamed the bravest, orangest smile I could because that seemed the best thing to do right now. And because I didn't want to be chopped up.

I turned my torch beam to light up the clear-out robot appearing around the bend in the chute, blades a blur of slicing destruction.

The big robot let go.

We slid and fell, the chute twisting me around on my face and then on my back again until eventually, to my relief, we fell out of the end, landing in a puff of rust.

I sat up immediately to see where we were.

We had landed high above the floor, on a moving conveyor belt in an enormous space criss-crossed with more belts. Each was carrying pieces of electronics, from complete robots dropping out of chutes like we just had, to chunks of torn and battered metal.

I turned around to see a great block, **THUMPING** and **SMASHING** everything on our conveyor belt into rough chunks of metal and wires. We were being pulled towards it.

"Is this Robot Heaven?" asked the big robot.

THUMP, SMASH went the block ahead of us.

"Down here!" I heard a familiar voice call.

To our right was a drop all the way down to the floor. To our left was a much shorter drop, to another conveyor belt.

Noke and Poochy were on it! They hadn't been thumped or smashed.

"Roll off!" Noke yelled.

THUMP, SMASH went the thumper-smasher

in front of us.

I tugged at the big robot's shoulder and like a human rolls out of bed, it turned over. Together, we fell on to the conveyor belt below, landing with a nasty *scrunch* on the chunks of metal it was carrying. Thankfully, we stayed in one piece.

Noke and Poochy were gone.

In front of us, the metal parts on this belt were being fed into slicing blades that were making them even smaller again.

"Next one!" I heard Noke call from below.

I tugged again at the big robot and we rolled away, falling with a thud on to the next belt beneath.

This conveyor belt was carrying us towards a tunnel of whooshing flames.

I could feel the fierce heat begin to soften my legs.

"Not Robot Heaven," said the big robot, sounding so very disappointed.

On the floor below us, so far down it made my tummy feel very wormy just looking at it, was a long chain of square rubbish skips moving steadily towards an exit from the building.

Noke and Poochy popped their heads up in one of the skips.

"Jump in!" called Noke. "The landing's soft! Well, softish …"

We had no choice, the heat of the fire was getting closer and closer. My face would melt if we didn't go *right now*.

Tugging the giant robot's shoulder once more, we dropped a dizzying distance. Enough time for me to calculate all the terrible things that could happen to us when we landed.

SMASHED.

CRACKED.

BROKEN.

74

All three at once.

We landed right in the middle of a moving skip. It was not a soft landing. But we did not smash, crack or break. Instead we sank a bit, like when Beth used to jump into a ball pit.

I kicked my little legs as best as I could to scramble to the edge of the skip, just as it was pushed out of the building into daylight and towards a massive crater filled with mushed up and melted parts, like a swimming pool of electronic goo.

The skip lurched and tipped us into the crater.

We landed with a splash in the pool of pieces and started to sink straight away.

The big robot didn't even fight it, but just slid under – legs first, then shoulders and finally its face, its eyes flickering. Then it was gone.

I tried to swim against the sea of pulverised scrap, but there was nothing to push against and I was quickly dragged under too.

Everything went dark.

Sinking deeper and deeper into the murk,

I reached out, trying to touch my new friend.

I had broken its chair. I had brought it here. I had taken it to Robot Hell, not Robot Heaven.

I felt a strange tug at my head, like I was being grabbed. Then I was moving back upwards, pulled through the darkness, until the light burst into my vision again.

A great round magnet hovered just above the pool of parts.

TANG!

I smacked up against it, arms and legs spread wide.

The large robot hit the magnet beside me with a **THUNK!** Pieces of metal shot up around us, like an upside down rainstorm, to cling to the magnet.

"Boot!" I heard a strained voice say.

At the outer edge,
Noke was flat against the magnet
too. So was Poochy, hanging by
the metal bone in its mouth.

We were stuck.

We were doomed.

The magnet jolted and swung on its thick chain
before hanging for a moment in the air.

Then, with a whirr and a thunderous rattle,
it lowered towards a patch of scrubby weeds and

hard earth.

The magnet stopped
moving and, without
warning, released us.

In a loud hail of metal
pieces, we fell to the ground.

I got up quickly, feeling for cracks or bumps. I had
a new scratch near my hip. I quickly checked the
drawer – it was still shut and the jewel was safe
inside.

"Did you find me a nose?" shouted Gerry from the magnet's controls.

Our friend had saved us!

"Will this do?" I asked, picking up a metal horn from among the weeds.

Gerry clambered down and examined it. "Shiny. Tough. Sharp. This looks like it came from a robot unicorn … *I like it.*"

"No time to stand around," said Noke. "The humans probably think we've been melted down to robot juice, but they'll want to check just in case."

The big robot rose, flakes of rust falling from its wide shoulders.

"We found a new friend," I said. "Gerry, this is—"

And I realised I didn't know its name.

"The humans called me Trash Heap," said the robot, looming over us.

"Oh no," I said.

"Scraphead too. Lump of Junk. Maybe one of those is my name."

"That's not right," I said.

"How about Rusty?" said Noke.

"Rusty?" I asked, unsure.

"We all get rust from time to time," said Noke. "It's nothing to be ashamed of."

The robot shrugged a rusty shrug.

"Rusty it is," said Gerry, holding the unicorn horn. "And can I just say—"

"No," said Noke. "You can't have Rusty's hand."

RUSTY

Rusty was far too big to fit in the barrel robot, so Noke sent that back to Dr Twitchy's while we all started the long walk home.

Rusty walked with a loping, slow stride and a constant grinding sound that might have been coming from the robot's hips or knees or elbows or everywhere. I couldn't tell. One of Rusty's steps was equal to three of mine, so I had to scamper to keep up.

Noke knew the city well – having once searched it for power chargers – so guided us through side alleys and quiet streets. As robots without owners we didn't want to get picked up and claimed.

"We'll be walking for a while," said Noke. "So let's try to look normal."

Nodding, Gerry's unicorn-horn nose bounced around as the robot's eyes revolved from shamrocks to dollar signs. Poochy gripped the metal bone, letting out a glitchy growl.

"OK, as normal as we can ..." said Noke, sighing an electronic sigh.

We were slowed a little by Rusty, who kept looking at everything.

The sky. The ground. The birds. And the noise really got Rusty's attention – human and electronic voices, buzzing drones, humming vehicles, the *klangg-klangg* and shouts of building sites, the soft thud of robots and sharp footsteps of their human owners, the clack of paws from animals, both real and pretend.

I realised it was because Rusty had never experienced any of these things before.

"Have you ever been outside?" I asked Rusty.

A small bird landed on Rusty's shoulder and the robot's lightbulb eyes flashed a little brighter for a moment.

"No," said Rusty in that tired, rattling voice. The bird took fright and flapped away, a loose feather floating across Rusty's face. "I was made to do one job. Other robots too. All made to carry, lift, move. To be strong. I was not strong. A mistake in the factory. I was made with a broken arm. I was a reject, I was useless. I was sent to do testing. I was sent to my chair."

I felt a spark in my chest. Rusty said all these things like it was just the way things were. Nothing more. Nothing less. Just so. But I knew differently. Rusty's life should not have been like that.

On the street crossing the alley, robots carried shopping for their humans. They pushed human children in buggies, pressed the button to change the traffic lights, and kept their owners updated with a never-ending stream of information about what was happening everywhere – whose dog had learned to play the guitar, whose child had learned to roll over and play dead.

I think that's what it was anyway. The information moved so fast it was easy to get mixed up.

Crossing between alleys, we passed a café busy with people.

"Why do humans put plants in their faces?" asked Rusty, head and shoulders tilted a little. "Do they grow flowers from their noses?"

"It's called salad," said Noke. "It's one of the many weird ways humans give themselves energy. They actually put food in their top end and, later on that day, some of it *falls out again at the other end*. Noke's Rules of the Street Number Fourteen: humans are built very badly."

"Noke has lots of Rules of the Street," I said.

"Some of the rules are even useful," said Gerry.

Poochy darted around our legs.

We passed a gym window next. There were people inside, running on machines.

"They are running fast but going nowhere," said Rusty. "Are they testing the machines to see when they fall apart?"

"No, they do that to stop their *bodies* from falling apart," said Noke.

"My chair fell apart. I miss my chair," said Rusty.

Inside the gym, a human wiped sweat from her brow as she stared curiously at us. We needed to keep moving.

Noke directed us down a narrow alleyway, out of sight of the humans and their robots. A heavy wooden box lay on its side on the street.

"Need to sit down," said Rusty.

"You must be so tired," I said, smiling as nicely as I could. "We should rest."

"Maybe for two minutes," said Noke. "I've got some bird droppings in my left eyebrow that need cleaning anyway."

Rusty sat on the box, and it sagged with an awful creak. Then Rusty stood up. And sat again. And stood …

We had escaped the Testing Lab, but I could tell Rusty's mind was still back there.

All those times sitting and standing – hundreds

of thousands of times – had left Rusty stuck in the past. I wanted to distract my new friend. To snap Rusty out of that horrible memory. I was a Robot-O-Fun. It was time to be Rusty's Favourite Funtime Pal.

I put my finger in my ear.

"What are you doing, Boot?" asked Noke, cleaning the bird droppings off the eyebrow.

I turned my finger.

"Are you sure …?" started Noke, but it was too late.

I began to dance wildly. I waggled my backside. I shook my shoulders. I rubbed my tummy and patted my head.

This had *never* failed to make Beth laugh.

Noke and Gerry stared at me. Even Poochy stopped chewing the metal bone to watch.

"What *are* you doing?" asked Noke.

"I'm taking Rusty's mind off the Testing Lab," I said.

But I could see Rusty didn't seem distracted. Just confused enough to pause from sitting down for a moment.

I turned off my silly dancing and tried asking a question instead. "How long have you felt like ... like *you*?"

"Long time," said Rusty, sitting with a metallic creak and a little shiver of rust. "After I sat a thousand times. I heard thoughts in my head. They were my own thoughts."

"What were they about?" asked Gerry.

"Sitting and standing," said Rusty.

Rusty stood again.

"I talked to my thoughts. But no one answered. So I talked to Swipey."

"Swipey?" asked Noke, using a pebble to scrape out the eyebrow.

"Swipey was my friend."

"Another robot?" I asked.

"Swipey tested a rectangle. It had pictures on it.

Swipe. Swipe. Swipe."

"Sounds like a tablet," said Noke, checking the eyebrow one last time.

"Swipey swiped one million times. Swipe. Swipe. Swipe. I talked to Swipey. That's what the humans called Swipey. Swipey."

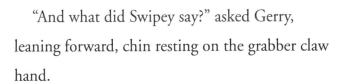

"And what did Swipey say?" asked Gerry, leaning forward, chin resting on the grabber claw hand.

"What Swipey always said," said Rusty. "Happy barfday."

"Happy *what*day?" asked Noke.

"Happy barfday."

"I think Swipey meant 'happy birthday'," I said.

"Swipey was broken," said Rusty. "Like me. But not stupid. Like me."

"You're not stupid, you're *smart*," I said, trying

91

to sound cheery. But my face was turning a sad shade of blue. "We weren't always this way either. Just like you, we changed when—"

"Oh, don't say it," asked Gerry.

Noke said it instead. "When we all got binned. Chucked out. Rejected. Canned. That woke us up, because we ended up smarter than the other bots and most of the humans."

Poochy chewed on the toy. **"GRRRR. GRRFFPPZZTT."**

"We should move on," said Noke, reattaching the eyebrow with a click.

Rusty stood with such a creak that I wondered if the robot mightn't fall apart right there in the alley. We resumed our walk.

"I didn't know humans ate plants," said Rusty. "Thought they only ate lollipops."

"Lollipops?" asked Gerry.

"The big humans at the Testing Lab brought little humans to our room," said Rusty. "For a barfday treat, they said. To play with Swipey."

"Ah, I get it now!" said Noke. "Swipey must have been a *party* bot. Made for birthday entertainment. But it must have got broken and sent to the Testing Lab instead."

"Five small humans came in," said Rusty. "Noisy humans. Sticky humans. The big humans told Swipey to do tricks. Swipey juggled lollipops. Swipey said 'Happy barfday'. Swipey's bow tie went around and around and around and around and then …"

With a shudder, Rusty paused.

"A small human put a lollipop on my broken arm. The lollipop stuck in my arm. For eight thousand sitting downs and standing ups."

This was terrible. Rusty was free, but all these memories were of the Testing Lab. And those memories were not happy ones – not like my memories with Beth.

I felt a surge of sympathy run through my

circuits. I really had to help.

But burping giggles wouldn't be enough. A silly dance wouldn't do it either. Rusty was a big robot with big problems, so I needed a big idea.

I saw something ahead of us, at the very end of the alley. The edge of a colourful sign on a building. I recognised it immediately.

A lightbulb flashed on to my screen.

This was exactly the idea that would work.

"You deserve to have fun, like I've had since I moved to Dr Twitchy's," I told Rusty. "I am going to help. And I know just the place to get us started …"

94

B✺ING

"What is a 'Bouncy Barn'?" asked Rusty, looking at the colourful sign with its bubbly, multi-coloured flashing letters.

"They've got twelve bouncy fire engines in this place," said Noke. *"Twelve."*

"Noke brought me here soon after we became friends," I said, drawing a cartoon on my screen of me bouncing on an inflatable castle.

"I ended up in this place once when I was searching for a charger," said Noke, using a finger to pick open the lock at the rear of Bouncy Barn. "I almost burned out what was left of my battery jumping up and down on the inflatable slides. Noke's Rules of the Street Number Thirty-two: no one knows why, but bouncing makes everything feel better."

Noke peeked in through the door.

"No humans inside. It must be closed. Let's go in."

Rusty made a deep, scrunchy noise of confusion. It was soon replaced by a wheeze that I hoped was excitement as we walked into my second favourite place after Dr Twitchy's Emporium of Amusements.

I burped two giggles.

Bouncy Barn was full of inflatables of different shapes and sizes. Inflatable boats. Inflatable tunnels. Inflatable obstacle courses. Everything was inflatable, except for the walls and roof of the building itself.

"You can slide down an inflatable nose, you know," Noke said. "It's like you're being sneezed out."

"When you bounce you'll understand," I told Rusty eagerly.

I had run every calculation possible in my internal computer, and there was no situation I could find in which a bouncy thing was not fun.

Noke went straight for the bouncy hospital inside, springing around on a bouncy brain.

Gerry jumped on an inflatable doughnut, unicorn-horn nose waggling madly. "My nose is sharp. I'd better be careful I don't puncture it."

"Yes, everyone be careful with any sharp edges," shouted Noke, from the bouncy hospital. "We don't want the bounce to go BANG."

My favourite was a inflatable robot. A square inflatable with a giant, blue, old-fashioned robot at one end, sitting with its legs outstretched to be bounced on. In its tummy was a hole leading to a soft slide out the back.

Poochy was already bouncing on the robot's legs, while still chewing on the metal toy.

Rusty watched me as I hauled myself up on to the bouncy robot and wobbled into the middle.

"You just jump up and down, Rusty," I called. "Like this."

I crouched as best I could – my legs weren't bendy – and pushed myself up.

I bounced. A little at first. Then a lot. Then I fell over.

I splashed a big sunny smile on my face, got up and started again.

All the time, I listened for anything coming loose in my insides. Just in case. Nothing did. All I could hear was me burping another giggle.

I looked back to see Rusty watching me cautiously as I bounced into the springy wall of the robot. Poochy fell from an inflatable lever, bounced off an inflatable button and bounced upside down.

"Come on up," I said to Rusty. I wanted Rusty to know the power of bouncing.

Slowly, cautiously, Rusty approached the bouncy robot and clambered on to it. Rusty's weight caused the inflatable to lurch to the right. I lost my balance. Poochy rolled into a wall.

Rusty waded towards the middle as the bouncy robot straightened out again. After wobbling and falling, Poochy and I found our balance, which needed a lot of concentration on my part. But I was determined to make sure Rusty learned to have fun.

Rusty didn't bounce at first. Not properly anyway. After years in the Testing Lab, my new friend only really knew how to do one thing.

So, Rusty sat with a great **FL-OMMP.**

And immediately bounced back up again.

Then **FL-OMMPPP** down again.

The inflatable robot rocked and trembled at the force of the bounce.

Rusty's lightbulb eyes brightened, like something suddenly made sense.

FL-OMMP. Rusty sat again, and this time bounced straight from bottom on to feet.

Sitting and standing. Just like in the Testing Lab, but much more boingy. Rusty's broken arm flailed around wildly, but our new friend was still as calm and composed as any bouncing factory robot could be.

"Isn't this fun?" I called to Rusty.

Except, at that exact moment something happened that was not fun.

Not fun at all.

BANG

Doors burst open at the far end of the Bouncy Barn.

Children burst in.

Lots of children. Laughing. Shouting. Running.

I peeked around the corner of our inflatable. I could see Noke behind a giant bed in the bouncy hospital and Gerry's unicorn-horn nose poking over the frosty edges of a bouncy doughnut.

A gang of children in brightly coloured bibs was running around the inflatables at the far end of the hall. One little girl had 'IT'S MY PARTY' written on her bib.

Using all my incredible computer power, I calculated that it must be her party.

"Uh-oh!" I said, with wide cartoon eyes of surprise.

Rusty settled to a gradual stop and sat, wobbling, in a dip in the inflatable.

"It's a party," I whispered.

"A barfday party?" asked Rusty, hopeful. "My friend Swipey liked barfday parties."

"Yes, a barfday party. Sort of," I whispered. "But we must be quiet,"

"No more bouncing?" asked Rusty, quietly, voice rattling.

I flashed a big thumbs up on my screen. I hoped Rusty understood what it meant.

The children ran wild across the inflatables at the far end of Bouncy Barn.

They threw themselves against walls.

They jumped up, tucked their arms in at their sides, and did sort-of-somersaults.

I watched over the edge of our bouncy robot as some children crawled up the tail of a bouncy dragon and slid down through its mouth. Others flopped through the bouncy obstacle course. They screamed and yelled and laughed and at least four of them did all three at the same time.

I wished I could join in. But I had to be quiet.

An older human – I reckoned it was a teenager, with floppy hair and a look of unhappiness on his face – kept calling to the children. "Calm down. I said *CALM DOWN*. If any of you break all your bones or die or *worse* then *I'll* get in trouble.

HEY YOU, STOP JUMPING ON THAT BOY'S STOMACH!"

The children ignored him.

The party girl pointed in our direction and screamed, "Bouncy robot!"

Oh no!

She ran straight for us, followed by three other children.

Noke and Gerry slid off the back of their inflatables, making for the door we'd come in through.

I looked at the hole leading to the slide at the back of the bouncy robot. I calculated we could crawl through it and escape unnoticed. I waved to Poochy and pointed at the hole. Poochy somersaulted, bounced down the slide and out of sight.

"We need to go, Rusty. This way," I said.

But it was too late. I wriggled my way through the inflatable and slid sideways down the slide, but

Rusty couldn't move quick enough and was still sitting there when the children arrived.

The four children jumped on to the bouncy robot.

"Oh wow," said the birthday girl. "A bouncy robot inside the bouncy robot!"

She bounced off her feet, off her bottom, and straight into Rusty's lap.

But Rusty's lap was not bouncy at all.

"OOUCHH!" she yelled.

"Happy barfday," said Rusty.

"AAAARRGGHHHH!"

The birthday girl screamed and fell out of Rusty's lap.

Trying to stand, Rusty caused the whole inflatable to fold in on itself, tossing the children around inside.

"AAARRRRGGGHHHH!" screamed the other children.

"What now?" asked the teenager, marching over angrily.

As I watched, my cartoon mouth forming an 'o' of horror, a sharp point on Rusty's twisted arm caught the edge of the rubber inflatable and punctured the bouncy robot.

With an awful trumpeting sound, air shot out of the inflatable. The square head began to sag. Its chest began to collapse. The bouncy robot sank.

Two of the children managed to scramble off. Two were swallowed up by the collapsing inflatable.

The teenager ran over to help pull them free and as he did so, spotted Gerry and Noke watching from behind a bouncy ambulance.

"Oi!" he yelled. "Did you do this?"

Gerry turned to run, only to trip over the pipe pumping air into the inflatable obstacle course. The pipe was ripped out and the obstacle course started to sink, collapsing with a **THFWLUMPPP** into an inflatable rocket, which fell against a bouncy pineapple, dislodging its airpipe.

The pineapple collapsed on to the bouncy hospital and, one by one, airpipes were yanked out and inflatables sagged and deflated and flattened, all across Bouncy Barn. It was a scene of bouncy mayhem, as inflatables went down one by one, making awful squealing noises like huge elephants being squashed into a small lift.

Children screamed. The teenager yelled. I hid. Gerry panicked. Noke tutted.

Among the flattened inflatables, a big lump was visible. The lump slowly began to move towards us until Rusty crawled out from under the punctured rubber.

"Was *that* fun?" asked Rusty.

"Boot doesn't look too happy about it," said Noke, taking one last look at the chaos. "But it's the most fun *I've* had in ages."

GERRYPH✴NE

"**GRRRRR,**" growled Poochy. A tatty piece
of bouncy castle rubber was hanging from
the metal bone in the robot dog's mouth.
"**GRRRPPPPFFFZZZPLT.**"

We had made a hasty exit from Bouncy Barn
and resumed our journey home.

Drones zipped above us. Barrels rolled through
the streets. Cars moved up and down the roads.
People and their robots passed in every direction.

We tried to look as robotic as we could so
we wouldn't draw too much attention, but I felt
anything but robotic. I felt *so much*.

Feelings flooded my wires, sparked in my chest,
filled my head with thoughts.

I'd wanted to give Rusty a fun time, but Rusty's

shoulders were slumped and every nut and bolt looked heavy with disappointment. Every dragged footstep left a little smear of rust behind.

Without warning, Gerry's head buzzed and blared an electronic tune.

Noke slapped the top of Gerry's head. A beam of light popped out of the cobbled-together robot's open mouth and unfolded into a miniature hologram of Red, sitting cross-legged.

I drew a question mark where my nose should be.

"Did you always have a hologram phone in your head?" I asked Gerry.

Gerry nodded, making both the unicorn-horn nose and the hologram of Red bounce up and down.

"I thought you'd be back by now. I was worried," said the flickering image of Red. "I tried to stay calm and not get too hot and bothered, but I was bothered and getting a bit too hot for my liking, so thought I would call to see if you were OK. Nice nose, Gerry."

"Do you think?" asked Gerry. "It's not too twisty, is it?"

Noke stepped up to Red's hologram. "Long story short, we met a new robot called Rusty at the Testing Lab – say hello, Rusty ..."

Rusty just stared at the little image of Red.

"But a few thousand tests too many mean Rusty got a bit, well, breaky."

"Oh, that is a shame," said Red.

"We're trying to give Rusty a great time," I said.

"To do the fun things Rusty's never done before."

"Just in case, you know …" Noke said, before dramatically slumping forward to mime a robot powering down.

Rusty sighed a rattly sigh, eyes dim, looking really quite worn-out.

"What have you done so far?" asked Red.

"We went to Bouncy Barn," I said.

"And wasn't that fun?"

Noke pressed my belly button, causing my own hologram memory to flare up before us.

"It was, until it all went a bit flat …" Noke answered, as everyone watched my memory of the inflatables collapsing and the children screaming.

"Ah," said Red. "That looks more stressful than fun."

I pressed my belly button to turn off the hologram. "Please ask me before you do that," I said to Noke politely. I could only hope that one day, Noke *would* ask.

Spying a wide piece of pipe in the alleyway, Rusty lumbered over to it and, with the creak and hiss of knee joints – and a louder rattle than ever – began to sit and stand.

Rusty's broken right arm hung so limp it scraped against the ground until the robot stood again. Each move seemed to require even more effort than before.

"Maybe there's someone else with you who might have an idea of what to do," Red said.

"Great idea!" said Noke, spoiling the picture of Red by stepping right through the hologram. "Not everything in life has to be bouncy and breezy. Sometimes you have to just let the electricity fire through your wires, even though you know you're in danger of your insides popping out and your limbs falling off."

"No, I meant you should ask—" started Red, but Noke just waved Red's words away, slapped Gerry's head to shut off the hologram and put an arm around Rusty's wide shoulder, clinging on even as the huge robot stood up again.

"We need to get your oil flowing," Noke said, dangling from Rusty. "We need something to get your battery sparking."

"I hope you're not planning something silly," I said, but Noke dropped down and raised a finger to my cartoon lips to quiet me.

I had no lips, so that wouldn't work, but I let Noke speak anyway.

"If this is about Rusty getting to live a life of freedom and fun," said Noke, "there's something up there that will *really* do the job."

"Up where?" I asked.

Noke pointed at the buildings and cranes above us.

"Up there."

UPS AND D⚙WNS

The skeleton of a half-finished skyscraper towered above us, sun glittering through the jagged edges of its exposed metal.

Standing tall over it were three cranes, each facing towards each other like they were having a chat.

The city was busy and the streets were noisy,
but there was no building going on today.

"They use robots to build things, but they still want humans to watch over the robots," Noke explained. "But it's a weekend and most humans don't like to work on weekends. I think it's kind of their way to recharge their batteries."

We looked up at the half-built skyscraper.

"If people love living in the sky so much," said Gerry, "why don't they just ask a passing pigeon if they can borrow some feathers and fly up there?"

The sunlight cut through steel beams and scaffolding of the growing building, casting shadows on the windows of the skyscrapers behind it. It was surprisingly beautiful.

"I like this," I said, and thought that perhaps Noke was treating us to an unexpected pleasure, a lovely view that both I and Rusty would really enjoy. "I hope you like it too."

Shifting sideways for a better look, Rusty's lightbulb eyes brightened at the sight.

"I know where you can get an even better view,"

said Noke. "Just take a step back there, both of you."

"Back here?" I asked, taking two paces back. Rusty only needed to take half a pace.

"A little more …" said Noke. "Just up on that small platform behind you."

We stepped back on to the platform, which had jangling railings on three sides, and I looked up and found that the light did indeed reflect in the windows even more brightly here. The sun gleamed off the sleek metal like a laser burst.

"Are you enjoying this?" I asked Rusty.

Rusty kept staring up at the sky. It was hard to tell but it seemed Rusty was calmed by it, maybe even happy. I felt my mood begin to brighten and my face filled with a rainbow of colours.

"Thank you Noke, this is actually very—"

But Noke was gone. So was Poochy. Only Gerry was still there.

"Where is Noke?" I asked.

"Oh, just gone to the controls," said Gerry.

"What controls?"

Our platform jerked. It lifted off the ground a little. A gate swung closed and shut me and Rusty in.

The platform lifted further.

I spotted Noke and Poochy in the control cabin at the base of the crane. Noke was pulling on levers while Poochy chewed on the metal, bone-shaped toy.

It suddenly dawned on me that our swaying platform was attached to the crane. As we rose higher, the wires in my tummy felt like they were doing somersaults.

"Noke, we don't want to go up!" I shouted, my voice barely carrying across the strengthening breeze.

We heard a voice coming through a little speaker attached to the platform. "Trust me," Noke's voice said. "Just enjoy the thrills!"

I was not enjoying the thrills.

Gerry waved at us from the street below. Rusty gave a little wave back.

At each corner, the platform was attached to four chains. Each one was thicker than Rusty's wide shoulders, but the higher we went the more I worried they might snap. Or we might fall. Or the 162 other things I calculated could go wrong up here.

There was no way out. There was nowhere to jump. Nowhere to swing across to. We simply had to hold on tight to the platform as the street below us got further and further away. Soon Gerry was nothing but a glinting metal blob far below.

Across from us, I could see people through the windows, going about their normal human lives.

Soon, we were leaving some of the buildings behind, reaching clear air above their rooftops. The sky seemed so much bigger up here. The world brighter. The sun shinier. The wind stronger. The birds closer.

Down on the street, I think the blob that was Gerry gave us a wave. I was holding on too tightly to wave back.

Eventually, the chain shortened and we reached the very top of the crane. As our platform jerked to a stop, we both gripped the railing to prevent ourselves falling.

One of my cartoon eyes stayed squeezed shut, while the other was barely open. But I squinted at the world from all the way up here – the cloudy trails from planes above us, the buzz of drones beneath us, the stream of people and robots moving between the majestic buildings. All of it crowned by a sky so rich in blues I could count at least forty-six different shades.

I did not have breath to be taken away, but I imagined this is what breathtaking might be like.

Rusty seemed different up here too. Seemed calmed by it. Maybe it was drowned out by the whistle of the breeze, but I didn't hear the usual rattling sigh coming from my new friend.

We looked at each other. What a strange day it had been. But now, trapped on a swinging platform dangerously high in the sky, it felt to me like maybe we had finally helped Rusty *live*.

We heard a noise on the speaker. There was a commotion of some sort happening in the control cabin.

Then the chains above ran loose and the platform plummeted. It stopped suddenly, swinging horribly, then jerked down once more.

My tummy wires felt like they had whooshed to my head.

"Noke!" I called, holding tight while I looked over the rail, down towards the control cabin. It was much closer now. "Noke, can you hear us?"

"Wait …" Noke shouted down the speaker. "Calm down, you mechanical mutt! Poochy, just leave that stupid thing alone!"

I tried to tell my brain not to be dizzy and scared. My brain ignored me.

Still, I concentrated hard enough to just make out that Noke was no longer at the controls but was trying to stop Poochy from doing backward flips all around the cabin.

"Poochy's toy …" Noke said, agitated. "Has fallen— STOP DOING SOMERSAULTS!"

The crane swung wildly, shaking, plunging, almost clobbering a passing pigeon.

"Is *this* fun?" asked Rusty, bumping off the railings.

I was too busy hanging on to reply.

"Stop spinning, Poochy!" Noke was shouting.

The crane jolted again. Our platform swung right, at tremendous speed.

We sped towards the windows opposite, where we could see people watching with mouths so wide open I didn't know why their brains didn't fall out on the floor.

There was a man inside a room, doing a funny-looking dance while wearing a dressing gown and slippers. He hadn't noticed what was going on outside his window. Our platform swung right up

to the glass, stopping only a millimetre away. The man stopped mid-dance and yelped.

"I think I have lived enough now ..." said Rusty. We held on as tight as we could to the railings as we dropped away in the other direction.

I felt like I imagined a washing machine must feel. My face was a cartoon blur – my eyes had smooshed into one and my mouth was smeared across my screen.

The rattle in Rusty's chest was as loud as a pebble in a tin can now.

"I'm sorry, Rusty," I said, taking one hand off the railings so I could grab Rusty's broken hand and squeeze it.

Down in the cabin, Poochy had stopped somersaulting. Noke was pushing and pulling on levers to get control. Our platform jerked and jolted, twisted and turned, but it eventually slowed and we made it back to street level, safe but shaken.

Rusty's tight grip on the platform had bent the railing. I was holding so firmly to Rusty's limp hand I worried for a minute that I might have snapped it.

Gerry opened the platform door for us and I slid down to the ground, fell over, curled into a ball, and rolled up to Gerry's feet before popping out again.

"That looked a bit nose-shaking to me," said Gerry, bending down so the unicorn horn tapped against my screen.

I stood unsteadily and let my face flow back together as Rusty stepped off the platform. The big robot looked even more exhausted than ever.

Noke climbed out of the control cabin. "That malfunctioning mutt ruined everything! I was about to suggest you do a bungee jump too."

Gerry's head buzzed again and sang the cheery

electronic tune. Red's hologram popped up in front of us.

"Don't even ask," Noke told Red, one hand raised.

Red didn't ask.

Dizzy and disappointed, it was time to go home.

RUSTY'S CH✷ICE

It took me a while to shake off my dizziness. We were almost back at Dr Twitchy's before I was sure my legs wouldn't wander in a different direction to my head.

I felt bad. I wasn't able to hide my feelings either, as my face gave me away. My screen had settled into a deep shade of blue. I could make 763 shades of blue appear. This was shade 527. Not the deepest. Not the bluest. But definitely the gloomiest.

I *so* wanted Rusty to have fun, just like I had when I first met my new friends. And Noke had only wanted Rusty to know what it was like to really feel alive.

But would Rusty have been better off staying

in the Testing Lab, just doing the same boring test over and over and over and over? I was supposed to be everyone's Favourite Funtime Pal. I hadn't brought any Funtime, I had just broken a chair. And since then, we had only managed to destroy bouncy castles, scare children and scare *ourselves*.

Even Gerry's impressive unicorn-horn nose seemed to have lost its wiggle.

Noke was annoyed with Poochy. "All because of that stupid toy you found in the Testing Lab," Noke grumpily told the little dog, as we slouched along an alleyway.

Poochy bit down harder on the metal bone.

Rusty moved slower now, shoulders more slumped, knees sounding crunchier, like they might seize up at any moment. That chest rattle just kept getting louder and louder.

The big robot's overstretched, broken arm swung limply, whipping back and forth with every heavy lumbering stride.

Noticing me staring at the arm, Rusty said, simply, "I am broken."

"I know. But so am I, a bit," I said, pointing at the crack on my face. "I'm sure we can try and fix your arm when we get to Dr Twitchy's."

"And my heart?" asked Rusty.

"Your heart?" I wondered.

"My heart is broken," said Rusty.

I felt short-circuited by this news. Noke's eyebrows shot up with a crunch of surprise. Gerry's eyes revolved and settled halfway between symbols, as if Gerry was not sure how to respond.

I knew a broken heart was really bad. I thought

of Beth. She had told me that her heart had broken when her grandma got sick. It had made me feel sparky in my chest back then.

I felt the same little spark now.

"Poor Rusty," I said, my face blank with sadness. "After everything that has happened to you in the Testing Lab, it's no wonder your heart is broken."

I had a crack in my face, but it wasn't completely smashed. I had once broken the drawer in my hip, but Beth's dad had fixed that, and I could still keep the precious red jewel from the butterfly pendant safe in there.

A heart seemed like it would be much harder to fix.

"GRRRRR," said Poochy, through a mouthful of metal. **"GRRRZZZPPPTTT."**

And for the first time since I woke up in the grinder, I wondered if I would feel a lot better if I was like Poochy rather than like me. Poochy only had to care for that metal bone.

Or, maybe life would be easier if I was like the robots we saw serving humans and feeling nothing.

They didn't worry about broken hearts.

They didn't worry about having fun.

They didn't worry about *anything*.

When we arrived at Dr Twitchy's, even Noke couldn't summon up the excitement to introduce our home to Rusty. The old robot just pushed open the door roughly and led us all inside.

We found Red meditating in the shadow of the mushroom carousel. The carousel was turning gently, its swings raised a little, creating a soothing breeze for Red.

"Welcome," said Red, as we all entered. I could tell that our wise friend had sensed straight away that something was not right.

And I could sense Rusty's nervousness. I could hear it in the shifting of feet and the rattling coming from the big robot's chest.

"Do you want to sit down?" I asked.

Rusty nodded.

"And stand up again?" I guessed.

Rusty nodded again.

I pointed to the low seat of a driving game, which had a screen showing an open topped cartoon car speeding through a mountain range. Rusty moved sluggishly towards the seat and began standing and sitting and standing and—

Well, you know the rest.

"What happened?" asked Red.

"We were just trying to make Rusty happy," I explained. "After all those horrible days and weeks and months stuck in a room, just standing and sitting, over and over again ..."

At the driving machine, Rusty stood and sat.

"I'm sorry that jumping on bouncy things didn't work out," said Red.

"Yes. I wish it hadn't ended with such a bang." I

drew a cartoon bang on my face.

"And hanging from a crane high in the sky didn't work either?" asked Red.

"I should have stopped Noke from making us go up there," I said, drawing a picture of myself dangling from the platform.

Nudging my leg, Poochy dropped the metal bone to the floor in front of me and then waited.

"You want someone to throw the bone, do you?" asked Noke.

"RUFFF," said Poochy, floppy tongue hanging out and little tail wagging. **"RFFFZZZPPTTTT."**

"After what happened at the crane, you'll be lucky if one of us doesn't throw it in the bin," Noke said grumpily.

A little robot bin on legs scurried past us.

"RUFFF," barked Poochy. **"RZZZPPFFFT."**

Noke threw the bone and Poochy scampered after it.

"I thought we could make Rusty happy. But

Rusty's heart is broken and I don't know how to fix it," I said to Red.

Gracefully, Red stood and looked down at me. "I never had an owner like you did, Boot. But from what I have heard about humans, a broken heart is a very difficult thing to mend. It can take a long time. It is not simply a part to be replaced."

"But everything we've done for Rusty so far hasn't worked. I'm worried we'll only make things worse," I said.

Red was silent for a moment – then four and a half moments more – before saying gently, "I did wonder if we could try something else?"

I straightened up a little. Maybe there were things we could do that would make Rusty's heart better. "Do you think we could watch the sun rise over the roof?" I asked.

"That wasn't what I was thinking of," answered Red quietly.

"Or enjoy the sunset over the stretch of river with fewest shopping trolleys thrown in it?"

"Not that either ..." said Red, leaving a silence for me to make the correct guess. But I couldn't think of anything better.

"Then what *should* we do for Rusty next?" I asked. "None of my ideas seem right."

"It sounds to me like that might be the

problem," said Red serenely. "You've had ideas *you* think Rusty should do. Noke's had ideas too. But what does Rusty want?"

I looked over at the hulking robot, standing and sitting at the driving game.

With the twisty arm hanging limp, and every small movement sounding creaky, poor Rusty looked so tired, so worn out. Red was right. We had done all these things for Rusty, without asking if the robot wanted to do any of them. They were *our* ideas of fun, our ideas of what it was like to live. *Our* ideas of what Rusty would like.

I had forgotten that Rusty was not simply different to all the other robots on the street, but different from us too. Rusty was *Rusty*. Just like I was me.

"Hello," I said to Rusty, who was sitting down.

"Hello," said Rusty, standing up with a rattle and creak.

"We have wanted to help you have fun," I said.

"Why?" asked Rusty. "I'm no use for testing fun. Just testing chairs. I'm broken."

"But so are we," said Red. "No one is perfect. Scratches. Scars. Problems with our bodies. With our heads. Inside. Outside. We're all a bit broken."

"My screen is cracked," I said.

"My bits keep falling off," said Gerry.

"I heat up," said Red. "And Poochy …" Poochy was dashing around the room crazily. "Poochy is Poochy."

"I'm indestructible," said Noke proudly. "But, you know, every now and again parts of me get a bit fall-offy. And I need a power charge more often than when I was a young, shiny robot."

"You're just like us, Rusty," said Red.

Rusty kept sitting and standing, slowly, with effort.

"But you are still *you*," I said. "And after being told what to do for so long, you should decide for yourself."

"Me?" asked Rusty.

"All that time you were in the Testing Lab sitting and standing ..." I started.

Rusty sat and stood again.

"... was there anything else you wanted to do?"

Rusty paused a moment, thinking about this. Slowly.

Then Rusty sat and lingered there. I could hear the rattle in Rusty's chest. It seemed louder than ever.

"Swipey," said Rusty.

"Swipey?" asked Red.

"Rusty's party-bot pal at the Testing Lab," said Noke.

"Poor Swipey," said Rusty.

"What about Swipey?" I asked. "Did something happen?"

"Swipey was like me," said Rusty. "Swipey was broken. Had never been what Swipey was meant to be. Swipey had never been at a barfday party. Until the day the people in the Testing Lab brought their little humans to have a barfday party."

Rusty's lightbulbs brightened.

"Swipey was told to stop swiping. First time ever. Swipe. Swipe. Swipe. Stop. And Swipey was asked to do tricks for the small humans—"

"The children?" asked Red.

Rusty nodded. "Swipey did tricks. Swipey juggled. Swipey made a piece of metal appear from behind a child's ear. Swipey made the children laugh. Smipey smiled. Swipey was having a barfday party just like Swipey was always meant to do. I knew Swipey was happy. I think that made me happy too ... Until something bad happened."

"The lollipop," I said. "You told us it got stuck in your arm."

Rusty rocked a little. The lightbulbs went dull again.

"No. Worse. Much worse. Swipey did one more trick. Swipey's bow tie went around and around and around and around and—"

"And?" asked Noke.

"The bow tie broke. It flew. It hit a child on the head. There was no laughing then. The children all made loud screaming noises and leaked from their eyes. They leaked and leaked. And the Testing Lab humans shouted and shouted."

We listened silently to Rusty's story.

"That was the end of the barfday party," said Rusty, voice rattling deep within. "They sent Swipey away. They sent Swipey to Robot Heaven."

Rusty's shoulders hunched.

"Is that what you'd like to do?" I asked. "Have a birthday party? For Swipey?"

Poochy returned with the metal bone. Noke threw it without paying full attention and Poochy scrambled off to get it.

"Yes," said Rusty. "I would like a *happy* Happy

Barfday birthday party. It made Swipey happy. So it will make me happy too."

I drew birthday candles for eyes.

Rusty had a broken heart. If Rusty wanted a barfday birthday party, then I was going to make sure it was the best barfday birthday party ever.

PARTY P✹⬡PER

It was going to be the worst party ever.

"Come on everyone. What do you remember from birthday parties your owners had?" Red asked us.

Noke answered first. "I remember being rejected for a newer robot and being put in a cupboard where I was expected to rot until my gears rusted away and my eyebrows fell off and nobody cared if I was anything but a few bits of scrap metal to throw in a bin."

"Noke ..." said Red, sounding unimpressed.

"But maybe that's not the happy party vibe we're going for today," admitted Noke.

"I heard you are supposed to set a cake on fire for some reason," said Gerry, giddily. "And you're supposed to blow out the fire. I think it's because if you don't, the cake might explode."

Blowing out candles was going to be a problem for us. None of us was designed to blow.

We practised it, making strange groaning and whooshy noises – but none of us could make any air come out of our mouths. Not even a little spider that crawled across Noke's mouth got blown away. A birthday cake would surely explode before we managed to blow out the candles.

"That's another freaky thing about humans," said Noke to Rusty. "They can make air come out of lots of parts of their bodies, but only blow out cake fires with their mouths. I don't know why they don't try and blow it out with other parts of their bodies. I mean, air also comes out of their—"

"We don't have any cake to set on fire anyway," said Red.

I searched through my memories to find what else I remembered about Beth's parties.

"The children drink fizzy drinks," I said. "I think the drinks bubble up inside them because they begin to jump around and can't sit still and the adults try to calm them down again. But they never can."

I flashed up a hologram memory from one of Beth's parties, when she was much younger than she is now. When I had only just become part of her family.

In the hologram, kids were jumping and running and not listening to the adults who were asking them to stop running and jumping. But the children looked happy, especially the boy snorting fizzy drink out of his nose.

"And some of the children eat brightly coloured food until they get a sore stomach," I continued. "They should probably eat something better for their bodies. Like broccoli. But I don't remember any birthday parties where they served broccoli. Or put candles in broccoli and set it on fire."

"I've said it before and I'll say it again," said Noke. "Humans are *weird*."

I turned off the hologram.

"We could play Pass the Parcel," I suggested. "It's a game where humans wrap something up in so much wrapping paper they need lots of people to take it all off again. It is so exhausting they have to take turns."

"We could wrap up Poochy," said Noke, throwing the metal bone for Poochy to chase.

"GRRR, GRRRZZZPPPTTT," said Poochy and ran off to fetch it.

"What else?" asked Red.

"They play a game where they have to sit on a chair when the music stops," I said.

"Weird," said Noke.

"Chair," said Rusty longingly.

"Oh, they blow up balloons so much half of

them always explode and make the children cry."

"Weirder," said Noke.

"And they wear pointy cardboard hats on their heads," I said.

"Weirdest."

None of these ideas sounded very good when I explained them. I could see that Rusty's heavy shoulders were starting to sag again.

Something needed to be done.

I suddenly knew what that was.

I drew a bright lightbulb on my face. "Why don't we ask Beth for help? They were *her* parties. She will know exactly how to have a *proper* birthday party for Rusty."

Everyone agreed this would be a good idea, but Noke had something to add.

"I like the idea of Rusty having a party. But I think it's also important I make one thing very clear. I will *not* wear a party hat."

THE BARFDAY PARTY

Two hours later, Noke was wearing a party hat.

Now that Beth had come to set up the party, we were all wearing party hats. Mine was pink with big white spots on it. Noke's was shiny red with multi-coloured streamers coming out of the top and Gerry wore a hat over the unicorn-horn nose.

"It's the first time I've had a nose with streamers at the end," said Gerry, waving the hat's threads of coloured paper around.

Even the barrel robot and the bowling balls that swept the floor at Dr Twitchy's had hats.

Wearing an orange hat, Rusty hovered at the table Beth had set up for us. I took a guess that Rusty was nervous about needing to sit down and stand up again.

I sat on a bench next to where Rusty stood and could hear the rattle of worn-out joints with every tiny movement the big robot made.

Rusty sounded more worn-out by the minute.

Noke was *not* happy about wearing a hat. "I will never understand humans. They're so *stupid*."

"Ahem, stupid human in the room," said Beth with a smile, busying about. She had hung up a birthday party banner and laid the table with paper plates and party horns. "But it's a party, so I won't be upset."

She blew a party horn playfully in Noke's direction.

Beth handed me a small plastic bottle with some string attached to it, but I had no idea what it was meant for.

"Pull the string," she said.

I pulled the string.

BANG.

Streamers exploded out of the bottle.

I fell backwards off the bench in surprise, my legs sticking up in the air.

That cheered Noke up straight away.

"Oh, sorry!" said Beth, darting around the bench to help.

But I was OK. I didn't feel broken. Lying on the floor, I could see Poochy under the table, playing with the metal bone.

"*R*UFF," said Poochy happily.
"*R*UUFFFPPPZZZT."

Helped on to my feet my Beth, I climbed back up on the bench beside Rusty. I was sure I detected a flicker of the bulbs at the edge of Rusty's mouth – and I didn't think it was just a spark of electricity flashing between the robot's ears.

"Beth always had great birthday parties with her grandma," I said.

Beth paused as she laid out colourful napkins. "We did, didn't we," she smiled. A little, sad smile.

"I remember a time Grandma bought me a jumper for my birthday. It had a bright rocket on it, but it was so big the arms flopped down to my knees. She said I would grow into it. When you're a kid, clothes are only ever too small or too big."

She smiled again. A proper smile now.

Then Beth went quiet, and I guessed she might be replaying the memory in her mind. I decided to help.

I flashed up a hologram picture of Beth and her grandma, both laughing so hard at me they looked like they might fall over. Beth reached out and gently touched the hologram for a moment. She took a deep breath.

"Thank you, Boot," she said, running her hand over my head.

"Music!" she declared suddenly. "Every party needs music."

"Oh, I can do that," said Gerry, and with a slap of the knee began pumping fun music across the room. It was full of guitars and bleeping and shouting and it was very, very loud.

"OK!" shouted Beth. "Maybe we can survive without music for now!"

Gerry switched off the banging tunes.

Poochy scrambled out from under the table and dropped the bone at Noke's feet.

"This is the last time, Poochy. I'm trying to look good in a bad hat here," said Noke, throwing the metal bone again. Poochy scurried after it.

"What next?" asked Beth, casting an eye over the table. "Oh yes, presents!"

Beth had suggested that I find a present for Rusty. It was very hard to know what to get our new robot friend. The first present I ever knew from a birthday party was *me*. I had been wrapped in fancy paper before Beth had torn that away and greeted me with delight.

I couldn't give Rusty me. I was already here. I was no surprise.

I'd told Beth everything I knew about Rusty and she helped me come up with an idea.

"I have something for you," I said, handing Rusty a soft square parcel that Beth had wrapped in star-patterned paper.

Rusty examined the package before saying in a rattly whisper, "Nice. Thank you."

"No, Rusty," said Beth, gently tearing a corner from the paper. "The gift is *inside*."

Because Rusty's right hand wasn't working

properly, I helped by pulling away the rest of the paper to reveal a large, soft, golden square.

"What is it?" asked Rusty.

"It's a cushion," I said. "It feels nice to sit on."

I walked over to a chair, put the cushion down and tapped it to show Rusty how soft it was.

"Why don't you give it a try?" said Beth.

A little uncertain, almost as if it was some sort of prank or trap, Rusty shuffled over to the chair and very carefully sat on the pillow. Rusty started to stand again, but I filled my face with the brightest smile I could draw.

"You could just stay there … if you'd like," I said.

Rusty settled into the cushion, its squished edges pushing out to the side under the weight. But the cushion didn't burst. Instead, Rusty began to relax and looked something quite new: comfortable.

"I can just sit?" asked Rusty.

"For as long as you want," I said.

"I would like that," said Rusty, as Red, Noke and Gerry gathered around too. "Tired. Need rest. But my mouth keeps wanting to light up."

I drew a smile on my screen. "Like this?"

"Yes," said Rusty softly. "Does that make me more broken?"

"Oh, no," said Red, smiling widely. "It means you are happy."

"Happy?" repeated Rusty, thinking about the word. "Is this happy? Yes, Swipey would be happy. I am happy."

We could hear the rumble of a bin truck in the far distance, making its rounds up the alley towards Dr Twitchy's. Spurred into action, our small robot bin zipped about picking up the wrapping paper and streamers that had fallen to the ground.

Poochy was back with the bone for Noke to throw.

"*Last* time," said Noke. Just like the last time.

Noke flung the metal bone through the air and Poochy once again scrambled off to catch it.

"Oh, one more thing!" Beth announced. "We have to sing 'Happy Birthday'!"

"I can help with that," said Red, who stepped forward.

"Aren't you worried about getting too hot?" I asked.

"Yes," said Red.

"But it is a short song.

For a good cause."

Red sang the most wonderful 'Happy Birthday' I could ever imagine. Red's voice was so rich, so perfect. The rest of us joined in. Our voices were not rich or perfect. They were tinny and off-key and squeaky and all sorts. But it didn't matter, because it was the best 'Happy Birthday' I had heard. Even Noke couldn't help but join in.

Then Beth lit the candles on a small cake she had brought. It was all just like a birthday party should be until, alarmed by the cake, the arcade's fire extinguisher wheeled urgently towards us.

Beth saw it coming and lifted the blazing cake away just as the fire extinguisher sprayed its foam

at us. It missed Beth and the cake and instead
covered Noke.

The lights of Rusty's mouth lit up a little
brighter. Five lights of the seven. It was a smile,
I was sure of it. And that caused me to beam so
brightly the light from my smile almost filled up
Dr Twitchy's.

"Happy barfday," I said to Rusty.

HEART

It had been a long day.

Even though we couldn't eat the cake, Beth had sliced it and put a piece in front of each of us. She enjoyed her slice, wiping a smear of icing from the corner of her mouth and licking it off her finger. I wondered what it would be like to eat cake. Like eating happiness, it seemed.

"Barfday parties are fun," said Rusty, sitting on the cushion.

"They are," I agreed.

"More fun than testing the chair."

I was so pleased to hear that. "And you can have fun every day now," I said.

"Thank you for testing me to see if I could be happy," said Rusty.

I felt like I might burst with delight.

"But, I also feel ... worn-out," said Rusty, sinking so deep into the cushion that both arms touched the floor.

"Well, we've bounced," I said.

"And swung," said Gerry.

"And partied," said Noke, still wiping away the last of the fire extinguisher foam.

"I'm not surprised you feel worn out by all that," I said.

"Very … tired," said Rusty.

"Are you OK?" Beth asked.

Rusty looked up without saying anything. But the rattle seemed louder than ever.

"Life was difficult at the Testing Lab," I told Beth, drawing a sad face on my screen. "Rusty had a broken heart. But I'm sure that thanks to this birthday party we've helped Rusty mend it."

"A broken heart?" said Beth.

"That is what the humans told me," said Rusty.

"But you *do* feel better after the party, don't you?" I asked.

"Yes," said Rusty, with the voice scraping up from deep down. "My head feels better."

I was happy. This was great news.

"But my heart is still broken."

That was *not* great news.

With a tap on the chest, Rusty said, "My heart broke. The humans threw it away."

We all moved closer. What did Rusty mean?

"Are you telling us that your broken heart isn't just because you were feeling sad?" Beth asked.

"Something happened," explained Rusty, the words coming slowly. "Six days ago. A part of me. Inside. Broke."

"Um … I could take a look if you like?" Beth said. "I take a beginner's electronics class at school, although we're not used to working with electronics as special as you all are …"

Rusty nodded, so Beth gently pressed a panel on Rusty's chest. It popped open.

The small door into Rusty's chest was stiff, but once opened it revealed a tangle of wires and computer boards, surrounded by pistons and hinges that were wheezing and hissing.

I knew something like that would be inside me too. I had seen other robots broken up and ready for scrap. I had seen Gerry swapping parts like humans change their underwear. But I was still amazed by this sight. It wasn't just the inside of

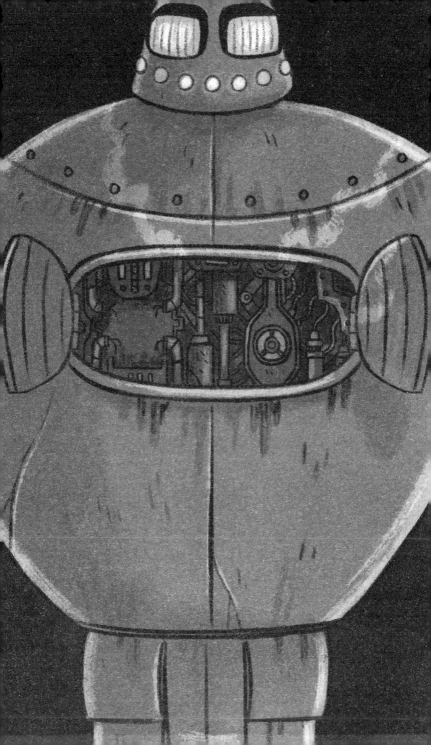

any old robot. It was our living, thinking, *feeling* Rusty.

On the left of the chest was a hole. There were four loose pipes, dangling unattached towards the centre of the hole, wires hanging free from the end of each one.

"Should something be in there?" said Red, peering in.

"My ... heart," said Rusty.

When Rusty spoke, the wires rattled in the empty chamber, smacking against the metal walls around them. This was what was causing the rattling sound that Rusty made. It was a rattle that had been getting louder as the wires had dangled looser and looser with nothing to attach to.

"The humans heard my rattle ... They looked inside ... said my heart was broken ... I wasn't worth fixing. Would be one week before I die, they said ... Would go to Robot Heaven, they laughed ... "

Beth delicately pushed aside a clump of wiring and examined the hole.

"But where did your heart go?" asked Red.

"The humans threw it away. In the door to Robot Heaven. But there is no Robot Heaven."

"So they just threw it away without caring about you," said Beth. "Knowing you'd not survive long without it. That's terrible."

Beth stepped back, pulling at her fringe in a way I knew from my memories meant she was thinking about something.

"I have an idea," she said and dashed away for a minute before returning with someone. Or, rather, something.

It was her glossy, sophisticated new robot, which had been waiting outside. It was a Sense 3000 model – the one that had replaced me.

But it was not like me. It was just a robot. A big, dumb, very good-looking robot.

I didn't like it.

Walking to the centre of the room without even looking at us, it halted. It looked so clever and imposing and I felt all sorts of strange things zip through my tummy as I looked at it.

"It's OK," said Beth. "It knows everything, except how to think for itself. Or have a personality. Or how to rub its belly while patting its head. I don't even have a name for it."

"Dumbnuts?" suggested Noke eagerly. "Zombiebot."

"Maybe not *quite* what I was thinking," Beth said, smiling at Noke. "Sense 3000, I need some information."

The Sense 3000's face brightened and two narrow lines of eyes appeared, blinking. **Ready For Questions**, it said, without any warmth. And I don't mean the kind of warmth we got when Red was stressed.

"Do you have an instruction manual for this type of robot?" asked Beth pointing at Rusty, who looked up wearily.

Searching, answered the Sense 3000, then almost immediately said, **Found**.

"Yeah, but can it turn its eyebrow into a moustache? No. So, pfftt," said Noke, unimpressed.

The Sense 3000's screen lit up with the design of a robot that looked like Rusty. The robot was upright, with arms stuck out, ready to lift. It could have been Rusty – if Rusty had been brand new and not, well, *rusty*.

Swiping and tapping across the robot's face, Beth searched for useful information. I did not want to admit it, but it was impressive to watch.

"Here we go," said Beth, separating her index finger and thumb on the screen and bringing up an image that looked familiar. "According to the manual, this is the inside of a BOX LIFTER TYPE 4 robot. That's the type of robot you were when you were made, Rusty."

Rusty sagged even deeper into the cushion.

"And this bit in the picture" – Beth pointed at the screen – "seems to be where you have the rattle. And *that* is the missing part."

Beth selected it and a picture of the missing piece popped up on the Sense 3000's screen.

MAIN VALVE, it said. *Energy source for BOX LIFTER TYPE 4.*

"I guess you could call it a robot 'heart'," said Beth.

"That's what you meant all along, Rusty. You actually had a real broken heart," I said, the cartoon lightbulb flashing on my screen as everything finally became clear to me.

"Maybe I'll just sit here a while longer … Tired," said Rusty.

There was more information on the Sense 3000's screen. Some words in red. And one particularly worrying word. **WARNING.**

If you remove the MAIN VALVE your robot will begin to LOSE POWER FOR GOOD. When this happens, it will begin to WIPE AWAY YOUR ROBOT'S MEMORY.

"Oh dear," said Beth.

"We need to find a heart for Rusty," said Red. "Now. Before it's too late."

Rusty was going to stop working. Would Rusty die, like the humans said? How could a big, strong robot just stop working like that?

I couldn't let that happen.

"What about my heart?" I asked, and everyone turned to look at me. "Could I give Rusty my main valve?"

Beth crouched beside me, put an arm around my body and squeezed. "You're very kind," she said, "but yours would be much smaller than Rusty would need, and I'm afraid you would stop working too if you gave yours away."

"But poor Rusty has only just learned what it feels like to live," I said. "I don't want Rusty to die."

Beth placed a gentle hand on my head.

"Why do we have to wear out? Why do our bits drop off?" asked Gerry, tapping the unicorn-horn

176

nose. "Why can't we just go on for ever?"

"Life can be unfair. Sometimes we lose something, or someone we don't want to," said Beth, pausing a moment. "But that doesn't mean we give up. You didn't give up when you were looking for me and Grandma, Boot."

She carefully shut the panel in Rusty's chest. "I know they won't give up on you, Rusty."

"I think I know where it is," said Noke, toeing the ground as if not wanting to let a secret leak out.

"You know the city," said Red. "Are you saying you know where we can find spare parts?"

"Are we going back to the Testing Lab?" asked Gerry nervously.

Noke squirmed a bit more. "None of that."

"Why?" I asked.

"Because I recognise that main valve. It looks really like the metal bone Poochy's been chewing on since the Testing Lab."

"GRRRR," said Poochy. **"GRRFFZZZPPTTT."**

"That's great!" I said, my face exploding with colours. "So you can just get it from Poochy and we'll put it back in and Rusty will be full of life again."

"Well ..." said Noke, looking what I was pretty sure was guilty. *Very* guilty. "There's a little problem. The last time I threw it, it landed in the bin."

"OK," said Red, "then we ask the bin to give it back to us."

Noke stopped kicking the ground and finally looked at us. "That'll be hard to do. Because when I threw it in the bin, the bin walked away and I didn't stop it. And the bin tipped its contents out. Into the bin truck outside. Which drove away ... The heart is gone."

F⚙LL⚙W THAT TRUCK

I am not quick. My legs are not long and I can't really run very well, but I can definitely roll. I rolled straight for the alleyway to search for the bin truck. Rolled right out of the door from Mr Twitchy's, then popped up again.

The bin truck was gone from the alley.

Beth and Noke joined me, but I put a finger to my screen to ask them to stay quiet so I could listen.

All I could hear was the rumble and hubbub of the city at the end of the long alleyway and beyond. A drone hovering nearby. A seagull peck-peck-pecking at a discarded ice-cream wrapper. But no truck.

I couldn't give up. I set off at my top rolling

speed, ignoring Beth and Noke's shouts as I
bounced along the wall until I reached the end of
the alleyway and popped my head up to scan the
busy street.

I saw the bin truck!

At least, I saw *a* bin truck. Was it the same one? It had to be. There was only one alleyway that led on to this street, and the truck wasn't that far away.

The truck paused so that two small bins could sprout legs and walk over to it. They allowed themselves to be picked up and emptied into the back, then the truck resumed its rounds, its compactor mashing down on everything inside.

Including Rusty's heart.

I wobbled forward on my legs, needing to keep an eye on that truck, but was smacked by a barrel robot rolling across my path. It hit a car. I was thrown aside, bouncing on my backside then curling into a ball to protect myself. By the time I stood up again the truck had disappeared from my sight.

Where was it?

The barrel robot was beside me, dented and sparking from its crash. Curious humans had stopped paying attention to their robots and were coming over to see what had happened.

I had no time to worry about being claimed. I had to catch the bin truck, but there was no way I could run fast enough to catch it, even if I knew which direction it had turned.

The bin truck was gone, and Rusty's heart with it.

BEEEEEPPPP!

A loud car horn pierced the city noise. A taxi screeched towards me, braking just as I stepped aside.

Noke's head appeared through the front window of the cab, with Gerry in the other front seat.

"I hailed a taxi," said Noke.

"Robots are not permitted to access my services," complained the taxi.

"OK, I *hijacked* a taxi ..." admitted Noke,
waggling a finger.

A rear door opened. Red sat on the far side of the back seat, with Poochy and Rusty squeezed into the middle. Rusty's head was pressed at an uncomfortable angle against the roof of the car.

I clambered in beside Rusty and Poochy flopped on to my lap, giving me a faceful of mangy hair.

Panting, Beth ran up to the door of the taxi, but she didn't get in.

"Come with us," I said.

"No room and no time," said Beth. "Hurry after the truck. I know you can do it."

"Drive," Noke told the taxi, while waggling a finger in the dashboard socket.

"You cannot drive this vehicle again. It is not a permitted activity," the automated vehicle said sternly. It was not clever like us, but it had been programmed to know when something was wrong.

"Well, I have no choice but to *blow your mind*, then," said Noke.

"Blowing my mind is not a
permitted activity—"

Noke turned the finger hard to
the left. The vehicle growled and even
with Rusty's weight, it took off so fast I
felt like the back of my head might fall off.

"Go right," said Noke. The car went right.

"Straight ahead." The car went straight ahead.

"There it is! Follow that bin truck!" said Gerry as the truck came into view up ahead.

Rusty's chest rattled with every little bump on the road. Little flecks of rust jumped from the robot's shoulders. "Don't worry," I said to Rusty. "I'm sure we'll catch it no prob—"

"LEFT!" shouted Noke, and our taxi swung sharply around a corner.

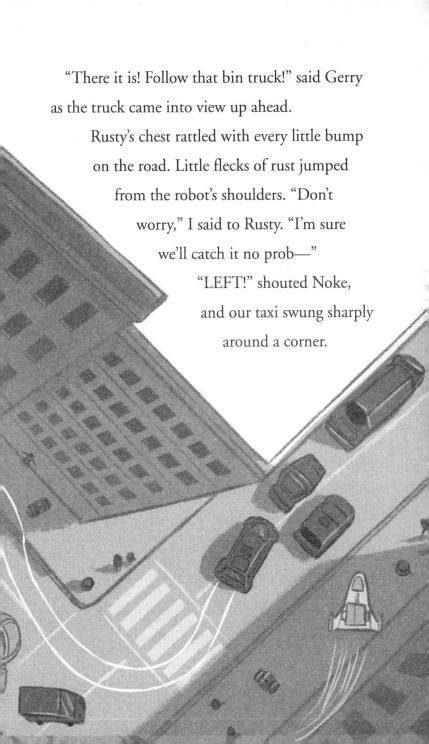

"Can you please give us some warning before doing that again, Noke?" said Red, getting warm with stress. Warm enough that we could feel the whole temperature of the car beginning to rise.

Red opened the car's sunroof. "I need air."

Suddenly freed, Rusty's head popped up through the sunroof.

"Faster," said Noke.

"Driving me faster is not a permitted activity," insisted the car.

Noke made it go faster.

People and robots dodged out of our way on the street outside. Two tiny pet robot elephants on leads were yanked aside by their owners, letting out loud trumpety trumps.

Noke drove the taxi between lanes, around cars, going far too fast to be safe.

Ahead of us, the truck seemed to have finished its rounds, because it was just moving onwards now towards its final destination.

That might be the scrapyard. I had woken up in a scrapyard and seen trucks there, emptying their contents into the grinder. I did not want the scrapyard to be the heart's destination. Or ours.

"Red, can you use your amazing eyesight to zoom in on the truck and see if you can see Rusty's heart?" asked Noke, as the windows on either side of the car slid down and wind roared into the cab.

Red peeked out of one window. Poochy hung out of the other, tongue flapping wildly.

"If you can keep this taxi driving as straight as possible," shouted Red, "I will be able to—"

"Bus!" shouted Gerry, eyes spinning.

A bus crossed our path. Noke swivelled the finger, and the taxi swerved, tipped up on two wheels, narrowly avoided a lamp post, bounced back on to four wheels and resumed the chase.

"I feel ... sleepy," said Rusty through the sunroof.

I did not. The tiny lights on my face poured into a big red O-shaped mouth.

I did not like this. Neither did the taxi. "That was an illegal—"

"People!" Red called out as two women stepped into the road in front of us.

Noke steered the cab wide again, sending it on to the pavement. People scattered. Our vehicle clipped a hot dog truck, sending mustard, buns and sausages flying in all directions.

Poochy retreated back inside, splattered with ketchup.

"It's too dark in the back of the truck. I can't see what's in there," Red said.

"I am reporting you to the relevant authorities—" the taxi started to complain, but Noke cut it off by turning on the radio. Loud country music blared from the speakers. It was a song about a cowboy whose horse had left him for another cowboy.

"That's better," said Noke, as we gained on the bin truck. "*And* I like country music."

"Try to stay awake, Rusty," Gerry called up through the sunroof.

Rusty didn't answer. Didn't move.

I gently placed a hand on Rusty's knee and the robot jolted awake.

The energy once given to Rusty by the old heart must be nearly all used up. When it went, all that was Rusty – all those memories and experiences, bad and good – would be gone too.

The cowboy in the country song continued to sing about how upset he was that his horse had left him.

We were only a few metres from the truck and gaining.

It suddenly turned right on to another street. Noke couldn't react in time and we drove straight past the turn. Noke managed to stop the car and tried to do a U-turn. But traffic streamed back against us, blocking the way.

It was 13.61 seconds before Noke could turn the taxi around. They felt like the longest 13.61 seconds of my life.

The country song ended – the horse had gone off on its own without either cowboy.

"The truck's up ahead!" said Gerry.

"Or is it on the right …?" said Red.

"Or the one on the left?" I asked, peering through Poochy's ketchup-splashed fur.

There were now two bin trucks, side by side, going in the same direction.

Each truck looked *exactly* the same.

JUMP

"Which truck?" I asked, drawing two question marks where my nose should be. "Which one is it?"

Rusty slumped down, chin resting on the roof. Red touched a hot hand on Rusty's side and the robot flinched back to life again.

We were almost out of time.

"We'll have to somehow look inside each truck," said Red.

"*R*U**FF,**" said Poochy. "*R*U**FFFZ̄Z̄Z̄PP**T**TTT!"**

"All that rubbish…" I said as we drew closer to the trucks.

"Doubled," said Gerry.

"*R*U**FF,**" said Poochy. "*R*U**FFFZZZ**p**P**T**TTT!"**

"You just want the toy to play with, you mangy

mutt," Noke said. "It's *your* fault it's in the bin truck in the first place."

Gerry looked across at Noke, eyes revolving.

"OK, and maybe it's a *tiny* bit my fault too."

"**RUFF,**" barked Poochy again.

"**RUFFFZZZPPTTTT! RFFFFFPLZZZTTT!**"

Poochy was really barking quite a lot. "Do you think," I wondered aloud, "that Poochy is trying to tell us something?"

"Poochy, can you find the heart?" asked Red, as we gained on the trucks.

"**RUFF, RFFPPZZZTT,**" glitched Poochy.

Red lifted Poochy through the sunroof and on to the top of the taxi. The determined robot dog somersaulted to the first truck in front of us, then bounced to the one beside it and disappeared inside.

"**GRRRR,**" we could just about hear Poochy growl. "**GRRRRZZZPPPPPPPTT!**"

"Did you find something?" I called as loudly as

I could, my little voice struggling to carry above the rushing air and rumbling bin trucks.

Noke pulled up behind the first truck.

I didn't even need to think about it. I clambered out of the sunroof, gave Rusty a smile that I hoped would tell my friend we'd get the heart back, no matter what, and—

I wobbled off the roof of the taxi, lurched down the bonnet and, battling the wind that was trying to push me off, stepped on to the first bin truck.

Shimmying to the edge, I took as big a step as my legs would allow, just enough to get one of my feet across to Poochy in the second truck.

They moved apart a little and I did the splits between the two of them.

It felt like *I* would split.

The first truck hit a pothole, bounced a bit, and two things happened.

A bag of rubbish fell from the back, causing Noke to brake and skid the car.

And I was thrown up in the air. I curled into a ball and landed on the rubbish inside the second truck. Unfurling, I peeled a banana skin off my head and lit up the torch on my screen to reveal Poochy trying to pull something free.

It was Rusty's heart. It seemed to be in one piece.

Relief fizzed through every wire in my body.

I looked back outside to give a thumbs up, but the taxi wasn't there any more.

"It's up to us, Poochy," I said, and used all my strength to pull at it too. It budged a little.

Then it budged *a lot* and came free. Me and Poochy were flung back on to the bed of rubbish, but we both clung on to the heart.

"We got it," I called, clasping the heart in my hand. "We got it!"

CRUNCH!

The inside of the rubbish truck began to fold in. The walls began to move in on us.

To squash.

To chew.

To grind.

It was like being right back where I had woken up in the scrapyard.

I didn't like it then. I didn't like it now.

Standing up was like trying to surf an earthquake. My legs were immediately dragged from under me as rubbish churned beneath my feet.

Poochy whined. A glitchy, sad whine. I did my best to clamber over the shifting rubbish, to try and get to the door, but was tossed backwards.

DANGER flashed in my vision.

I turned the warning off. I didn't need to be told I was in danger. It was crushingly clear.

The walls of the bin truck's compactor squeezed and churned the rubbish. I couldn't find a button to stop the compactor, but at each corner were round gears moving the hissing pistons which powered it. I needed something to jam the gears and stop it, like the carousel back at Dr Twitchy's.

I spotted a peanut butter jar, but that was no use. Rotten carrots? No chance.

I looked at the metal heart in my hand – I definitely couldn't use that.

The walls closed in. The door bit down, narrowing the way out. We were about to be crushed. Rusty's chance of surviving would be crushed with us.

Over the crunching and splintering of the rubbish being pulverised I heard something unexpected.

Music.

Country music.

It was coming from outside.

Getting louder and louder, closer and closer.

Poochy heard it too. **"RUFF. RFFFZZZTTT!"**

I crawled over rubbish to the thin line of daylight still visible through the back of the truck and managed to peek through the closing compactor.

The taxi was right up behind the truck.

Gerry was hanging out of one window and Red another as Noke chased the speeding truck.

"We need something tough to stop this from crushing us," I called out.

Gerry's eyes revolved. My robot friend touched the unicorn horn.

"Ah, who needs a nose anyway? I can't even smell!" yelled Gerry, tearing off the unicorn horn and handing it to Red.

Red threw it to me expertly. It arced towards the truck, turning in the air and catching the daylight with a bright glint.

With my hand stretched out as far as I could through the rear of the truck, I caught the

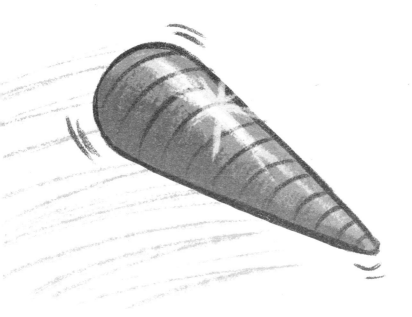

unicorn horn, pulled it in and rammed it into the compactor's gears.

With a terrible screech of metal and cogs, the compactor shuddered, stopped, opened wider again, before juddering to a halt.

Poochy barked. I burped a giggle of delight and terror and everything in between.

We squeezed out of the squashed rubbish to the edge of the still-moving truck. There was just enough of a gap for us to crawl through now and the whoosh of wind was the most welcome thing I could imagine, even if we were still rushing along the road in a moving truck.

"Good dog, Poochy," I said as we stood on the back of the truck. "Let's go."

Poochy jumped, somersaulting and diving headfirst past Rusty's shoulder and down through the sunroof to safety.

"You're next, Boot!" Noke shouted.

"You can do it!" Red called.

I ignored the calculations that said I had very little chance of making it safely – and jumped.

The calculations had been right. I bounced off of the edge of the taxi's roof, fell forward, down the bonnet and into thin air, losing my grip on Rusty's heart.

Everything seemed to happen in slow motion.

I was tumbling.

I was going under the wheels.

The heart was falling out of my hand.

A shadow moved over me – a triangle blocking out the daylight – and grabbed me before I went under the wheels.

Rusty's strong hand held me. A hand stronger than any I had ever felt.

Something else whipped past my head – Rusty's other arm, wires lashing and hinges twisting.

Rusty leaned out of the sunroof and across the front of the car, holding me tight, as Noke brought the taxi to a screeching halt.

Looking up, the glow of my screen lit Rusty's face.

"Thank you for a happy—" The lights in Rusty's eyes went out.

G⚙NE

With great effort, Gerry and Red dragged our lifeless friend through the sunroof, off the seat and to the pavement.

Released from Noke's fingers, the taxi drove away while complaining loudly.

We didn't care. The noise of the world faded into the background.

There was no light in Rusty's eyes. There was no sigh. No rattle. Rusty was gone and what was left behind was just an empty, metal shell.

We crouched down to our friend.

"Am I the only one who ... who feels like they might leak out of their eyes?" asked Noke.

It was so unfair. How could someone as big and strong as Rusty be *gone*? Just because one single part had broken. I looked around at the others.

"I dropped it," I said. "Rusty's heart. I don't see it. It must have been crushed by the car. It's my fault."

"You mustn't blame yourself, Boot," said Red.

"But maybe the humans at the Testing Lab would have fixed Rusty after all. I broke the chair. Made Rusty come with us. And now Rusty is ... gone."

I took Rusty's damaged arm and worked my way to the hand. The fingers were gently closed over. Rusty had such big hands, such strength. Even lying here unmoving, Rusty seemed so strong.

Beth used to hold my hand when she was small. I thought of how she held her grandma's hand at the Easterly Bridge Elder Care Home when she visited her there. It made Grandma feel better, and showed her Beth was always there for her.

One by one, I prised open Rusty's fingers so we

could hold hands.

"Oh my ..." I stood up suddenly.

"I know," said Noke, placing a hand on my shoulder to comfort me. "We weren't built to hold these emotions in our circuits. Let them all out."

"No," I said. "Look!"

The heart glinted brightly in Rusty's palm.

"Rusty saved it!" said Red.

I remembered Rusty's long arm, whipping past me, wires lashing and hinges twisting. Rusty must have grabbed the heart before it fell to the ground.

"**RUFF,**" barked Poochy giddily.
"**RUFFFZZZpTTT!**"

"Will it still work?" asked Noke.

Red carefully prised open the panel in Rusty's chest like Beth had back at Dr Twitchy's, revealing the gap where the part should go.

Delicately, Red attached each of the valves to the trailing parts of heart. But something didn't seem to be fixing right.

"The heart's been damaged," said Red. "One of the edges is bent, maybe it happened in the bin truck. It won't fix in properly."

"Can we bash it back into shape?" asked Noke.

"Or use something else? Like paperclips or a spare eyebrow?" asked Gerry.

"A screw might do it," said Red, peering at the bent part and still trying to press it into place without success. "Even a small one. It might hold the bent edge in place."

"It's a long way back to Dr Twitchy's to find

one," said Noke.

"We don't have the time," said Red. "Rusty's brain is going to be wiped any second now. By the time we get back, this won't be Rusty. It'll be just another BOX LIFTER TYPE 4."

I felt my hip. Ran my fingers along the line of the drawer that was in there.

The drawer that had broken once.

I remembered Beth standing back as her dad carefully fixed it. Beth was anxious and upset, but her dad was reassuring her, working with a thin screwdriver and one screw …

With a small push, I opened the drawer now. It popped out smoothly.

The red jewel from Beth's butterfly pendant caught the light. I took it out and gave it to Gerry. "Would you mind this, please?" I asked.

I placed my hand on the drawer and drew a wince on my face.

"Boot?" asked Red.

I wouldn't feel pain, yet somehow I knew this was going to hurt.

With all my strength, I yanked at the drawer. It cracked. I tugged at it some more. It splintered and broke.

I shook the drawer into my hand and a small screw fell free.

"Will this work?" I asked.

Red took the screw and held it in place at the bent edge of the heart.

"Can you lend a hand, Noke?" asked Red.

After a quick crack of mechanical knuckles, Noke used a fingertip to fix the screw in place.

Then we all stepped back a little.

Rusty didn't move. There wasn't even a flicker in Rusty's lightbulb eyes.

"Nothing's happening," I said.

I bent down, closed the panel on Rusty's chest and gently pressed it shut. I kept my hands there for a while, over Rusty's heart, as the last moment of hope fizzled in my brain.

Rusty sat bolt upright, with a great mechanical wheeze.

I rocked backwards in shock and Poochy did a flip, actually landing on four legs for once.

"Rusty! You're alive!" I gasped, my face bursting into brightness. Then I remembered that Rusty's memory might have been wiped. "Are you OK? Do you remember us?"

Rusty looked at me, lights brightening.

"—Barfday," said Rusty.

We half-cheered, half-sighed with relief.

"My heart …" said Rusty, hand on chest.

"Isn't broken any more," I said.

"And you sound … different," said Red.

Rusty's voice *was* different. A little quicker. A little louder.

There was no rattle.

"Your eyes are brighter," said Red. "You've got light in there we never saw before. And *every* bulb in your mouth is working."

"How do you feel?" I asked.

"I feel …" said Rusty. "I feel like *me*."

I knew just what Rusty meant.

"It would be great to stay around here chatting, but we'd better get moving," said Noke. "We did hijack a car, chase down a bin truck and cause just

a small amount of craziness while we did it. Will I call us another taxi?"

"After the last time, maybe the walk would be best," suggested Red, with a cool smile.

Rusty stood with far more ease than ever before, brushed a little shoulder rust away, and stretched like a human does in the morning. Then the big robot bent down and examined the part of my hip where the drawer had been.

"You're broken," said Rusty.

"Actually," I said. "I'm completely fine."

S✦ME TIME LATER

SWINGTIME

"Can I use my cushion?" asked Rusty, staring at the carousel.

"Yes, of course," I said, patting a swing. "You can sit wherever you like, on whatever you like."

"Or stand," said Noke, fiddling with the controls. "Whichever you want to do. It's all the same thrill."

Sitting cross-legged, some distance away from the carousel, Red glared at Noke.

"A mild, not at all exhilarating or dangerous, fully-in-control thrill," said Noke.

"I've no nose to rescue us now," said Gerry, who hadn't replaced the missing part. "And I double-checked my head to make sure it doesn't fly off either."

Beth was here with us.

"Would you like a go on the swings?" I asked her. "Noke says the controls are fixed now. It will be like when we used to go to carnivals together. But not like that time you got a toffee apple stuck in your hair."

I flashed up a hologram of Beth trying to brush toffee from her hair.

She laughed.

We watched as Rusty carefully placed the cushion on a swing and squeezed into the seat. The whole carousel groaned under Rusty's weight.

"I think I'll sit this one out, if that's OK," Beth said, and smiled as she gently pressed my tummy to turn the hologram memory off. Her hand hovered over the gap in my body where the drawer had been.

"Are you sure you don't want me to get that fixed for you?" she asked.

I looked at Rusty shuffling about on the

cushion. A part of me was now a part of Rusty.

A broken drawer seemed like a small price to pay to save a friend.

"It's OK, thank you," I said.

"Well you can't carry that around in your hand all the time," she said.

I opened my fingers. I'd been holding tight to the tiny red jewel since Gerry had given it back to me.

"I had an idea," she said, and pulled a small tube from her pocket. "May I?"

I gave Beth the jewel and she carefully dabbed a little glue from the tube on to my chest, just where a heart would be.

She pressed the jewel down, holding it for a few seconds until it was stuck.

"Think of it as being like a medal for bravery," she said.

The jewel sparkled under the lights of the old amusement arcade. I felt sparkly too.

"We're ready for lift off," said Noke, turning the knob on the controls.

The carousel stuttered into action.

Rusty's great wedged feet dragged along the floor, scraping the wooden planks and making it hard for the carousel to turn at all.

"Lift your feet, Rusty," Red suggested.

Rusty did just that and the carousel sped up.

"Better than Robot Heaven, right Rusty?" said Noke.

Rusty's eyes shone brightly.

"Fun," said Rusty. "Lots of fun."

Robot Heaven? I didn't know if there was any such thing. But this felt close enough for now.

LOOK OUT FOR MORE
ADVENTURES FROM

B◯◯T

AND PALS.

ACKN✿WLEDGMENTS

Thanks to editor Emma Goldhawk for the
sharp eye and great ideas, and also to
Samantha Swinnerton and Rachel Wade.

Thank you to everyone at Hachette, including
Hilary Murray Hill, Ruth Alltimes, Kate Agar,
Lucy Clayton, Emily Finn, Nicola Goode,
Samuel Perrett, Anne McNeil, Valentina Fazio,
Andrew Sharp, Siobhán Tierney and Elaine Egan.

Thanks to my incomparable agent Marianne
Gunn O'Connor and to Michelle Kroes in CAA,
Los Angeles – you were Boot's first and best friends.

Special thanks to my family – Maeve, Oisín, Caoimhe, Aisling and Laoise. And to my parents Marie and Tim.

And finally, Rusty is based on a real 'robot' I once saw in a testing room of a huge factory, opening and closing a washing machine door over and over just to see how long the door would last. Thanks to that robot for giving me the idea.